Meyer never expected to become a member of a pack of wolves. He's a vampire, and wolves and vampires notoriously hate each other, yet here he is, peacefully living with the pack.

Well, mostly peacefully.

Ollis never took things too seriously until his pack became the target of the dragon clan. His family still sees him as an immature teenager, even though he outgrew that phase a while ago. When his alpha asks him to step up and help guide the pack, Ollis readily agrees. No matter how frightened he is, he'll defend his home.

And he won't do it alone.

The pack is still at a disadvantage, but they have something the dragons don't.

Each other.

Resolute Fangs

ISBN: 978-1-4874-4149-4
Cover art by Angela Waters

Published by eXtasy Books Inc

Look for us online at:
www.eXtasybooks.com

Resolute Fangs
Life with Fangs 12

By

Catherine Lievens

Chapter One

"Do I really have to do this? No offense, but I have better things to do," Alpin said.

Meyer wasn't impressed. He stared at his brother, not one bit surprised by Alpin's answer to their father's question.

Tyrian had infinite patience, which he needed when it came to Alpin. It had also served him well with his partner, and it was good to see him happy with Madison. Now if only the dragons would stop trying to kill the pack, everything would be peachy.

Tyrian shook his head. "You don't have to guard Luca if you don't feel like you can, but the entire family needs to work on this. The pack needs us."

Tyrian was patient, but he was also smart, and he knew Alpin. Insinuating that Alpin couldn't do something was the best way to push him to do it. People tended to underestimate him, which was understandable. He looked like an angel, with his blue eyes and blond hair.

But he was a devil inside.

Sure enough, Alpin crossed his arms over his chest. "I never said I couldn't do it, just that I didn't *want* to do it."

"That's fair, too. We can find you something else to do."

"No, it's fine. I'll keep an eye on the dragon when you need me to. I'm not spending the nights here, though. I have a boyfriend."

Meyer grinned at Parker, who was standing next to him by the living room wall. Parker bumped their shoulders together, then turned his attention back to Alpin. "Everyone knows you have a boyfriend. I don't understand why Merrick puts up with you, though. Are you paying him?"

Alpin stuck his tongue out. "I'm pretty sure he doesn't understand why he does either, but it doesn't matter. He's stuck with me."

Meyer laughed. Alpin might be bratty, but deep inside—very deep inside—he was a sweetheart. He'd help anyone who needed it and was ready to sacrifice a lot if it meant the pack won this war. It was his home now, and he'd defend it.

Meyer still wasn't sure what he'd do after this was over. He supposed it depended on how things would end. He didn't have anyone keeping him here like Alpin, Tyrian, and Mallory. They'd all found someone to love here, but Meyer hadn't. He was happy for them, but sometimes, it felt lonely, even with his many siblings. Brothers and sisters couldn't give him what a partner could.

"If the three of you are done, someone needs to keep an eye on Luca," Tyrian said, glaring at Alpin and Parker.

"I'm busy right now," Alpin quickly said, moving toward the door. "I promised I'd meet Merrick, and he wouldn't be happy if I didn't go. You know how grumpy he is when he's unhappy."

"He's always grumpy," Parker muttered.

"And *that's* why I need to spend as much time as I can with him," Alpin said with a grin. "Tyrian, text me when you need me to stay with Luca, and I'll be there. Maybe try to choose times when Merrick is busy, all right?"

Alpin didn't wait for an answer. He hurried out of the door, leaving the three men in the room to stare at his back.

"I'm surprised he agreed," Parker said lightly.

"I'm not," their father said. "I didn't expect any of you to refuse. The pack is our home now. Every one of us will do whatever we can to defend it, including Alpin."

Maybe especially him. He had Merrick, and as long as the

dragons were a danger to the pack, they were a danger to Merrick. That would be enough for Alpin to want to do what he could to ensure his boyfriend was safe, including guarding the dragon no one trusted.

Meyer certainly didn't, but he also didn't think Luca would try anything nefarious. Meyer didn't know the dragon, but something told him Luca really wanted to help.

How was what Luca had done any different than what Merrick and Arlen had done? The two of them had left the dragon clan and were fighting them. Luca might only have left the dragons recently, but that didn't mean he was a spy or that he'd go back to them. The clan was doing enough damage that most people didn't want anything to do with them. Many of the clan members were probably stuck there, but Luca had escaped, and he'd come here knowing he might not be welcome. That had taken a lot of courage, and Meyer admired that.

But now they were stuck babysitting the dragon until people trusted him, and there was no way to tell how long that would take. Unlike Alpin, Meyer didn't have anything better to do, and he certainly didn't have a boyfriend, but that didn't mean he wanted to babysit any longer than the others. The dragon was sexy as hell, but that wasn't enough for Meyer to want to spend time with him.

Parker pushed away from the wall. "Well, I'm going upstairs to keep an eye on Luca, then," he told Tyrian. "Just text me to warn me when I'll be replaced."

"I'm still trying to set up a schedule, but I will. I'm heading out to meet Kieran and Sloan right now, but I don't think I'll be gone long, so I can take over later if you need me to."

"You know where to find me."

Parker left the living room. Meyer quickly followed him, his thoughts on Luca and what he'd done.

There was no way every member of the dragon clan was

okay with what their alpha was doing. It wasn't only the drugs that killed supernatural creatures anymore. The clan had attacked a mall full of humans, destroying it and killing many people as they did so. It meant that the humans were aware of the existence of the dragons now, and they'd been hysterical since the attack. They wouldn't find the dragons unless they wanted to be found, and if they ever did, there was no way it would be a good thing.

"What do you think of Luca?" Parker asked.

"I believe he wants to help us."

Parker nodded as if he'd expected Meyer to say that. "I feel the same. Do you think Kieran will ever be able to trust him?"

"I don't know. Luca was at the mall when it was attacked, but as far as I saw, he didn't hurt anyone. It's a bit of a coincidence that he reached us then, but maybe the attack was the distraction he needed to escape. Honestly, I don't know if we'll ever be sure he's on our side. He could be a spy planted by the dragons."

"We've just gone through that with Madison. I hope that's not so."

Meyer had to agree. Madison, Tyrian's boyfriend, had been forced by his father to follow the group of wolves who'd left the pack. They'd followed the alpha's sister, Fay, and since they'd left, they'd been trying to get back at Kieran and the pack. Fay wanted to be the alpha and had sent Madison in to spy on the pack and her brother. Unfortunately for her, Madison was honest and had told Kieran everything. They'd managed to get his sister back, so Fay had nothing to force him into spying for her anymore.

But Luca wasn't a wolf shifter. He was a dragon, and he didn't work for Fay. The dragons might have sent him to spy, but it didn't feel like something they'd do. They were more the type to attack and destroy first, ask questions and find information later.

Which was a massive problem.

Meyer and Parker reached the door of the room where Luca was being kept. It was the same room where Madison had stayed when he'd first arrived, and it felt odd to have a bedroom designated to hold prisoners. Meyer had never considered himself a prison guard, and he hoped this wouldn't last too long.

He wanted this war to be over and for people not to be hurt anymore. As long as the dragons had their sights on the pack, that wouldn't happen.

"I really wish people were willing to listen to Luca," Parker said.

There were two chairs in the hallway, and Meyer flopped into one. He narrowed his eyes at his brother, already knowing that whatever Parker was feeling, it was a bad idea. "I might not believe that Luca is trying to hurt us, but it doesn't mean you have to fall for him."

Parker's cheeks flushed as he shook his head. "I'm not falling for him. I barely know him."

"But you're intrigued."

"Aren't you? Luca has a lot of answers, but no one's asking him questions."

"They will eventually. The situation is complicated enough without adding you having a relationship with Luca to the mix."

Parker set his jaw. Meyer had said what he needed to say, so he didn't try to push his brother. Parker would do whatever Parker wanted to do. He'd always been like that, and he could never change.

"Maybe we should have gone with Fay," Malcolm said.

Ollis froze. He couldn't believe his brother had just said that.

Actually, he could believe it. Malcolm was an asshole on the best of days.

Ollis kept his hands wrapped around his cup of coffee and looked around at his family. They'd met in the kitchen in the house where Ollis had grown up. Sometimes Ollis missed it, but then he spent time with his brother and realized that he really didn't. The less he saw Malcolm, the better he felt.

Their father seemed to feel the same, at least when it came to what Malcolm had said. "Don't you dare talk like that," he snapped. "She betrayed our alpha."

Malcolm raised his hands. "I know the old alpha wasn't great and that Kieran is doing a better job, but still. We're all in danger, and it's not just wolves or bears that we're facing. These people are dragons, and they're dangerous. Do you really think we have any chance to beat them?"

"I do," Ollis said. "We have dragons on our side, too, and Kieran is working hard to find more allies. No one wants the dragons to take over the city. They just need to realize it's time for them to do something about it and help us."

The pack had been right in the middle of it since the beginning, and it was starting to take its toll. It wasn't only Malcolm. Ollis had heard several people grumble about the way Kieran was leading the pack and wondered what would have happened if his father were still the alpha. Ollis might be young—although he wouldn't call himself that since he was in his late twenties—but he'd seen the way Kieran's father had led the pack. It hadn't been good for anyone except Kieran, and not having him here was good. It meant the pack wasn't picking stupid fights with other packs, which was the last thing they needed, considering the dragons were gunning for them.

Malcolm shook his head. "You don't understand because you don't have a family," he said. "Things would be different if you had children to protect."

Ollis was offended but not surprised. Malcolm always thought he was better than everyone, especially his younger brother. It was bullshit, but Ollis had learned to live with it. He wasn't about to let Malcolm use the fact that he didn't have children against him, though.

"I don't need to have children to want the pack to be safe. Do you think I want to lose you? Or Mom and Dad? I don't want anyone in the pack to be hurt by what's happening, but I'm not going to hide my head in the sand. We won't be able to avoid a war, which has nothing to do with Kieran and how he's leading the pack. The dragons are going to fight us, and I don't think anything will change their mind. The only thing we can do is get ready to defend ourselves when they attack."

Malcolm was shaking his head again. "I know that, but trust me, things would be different if you had kids. This just shows that you need to grow up. You should already be married and have children. I was at your age."

Ollis gritted his teeth. He looked at his parents, but he knew neither of them would step in. They never did.

They probably thought Malcolm was right. Malcolm had gotten married in his early twenties and had started having kids right away. He had three now, and they were the joy of Ollis's parents' life. They loved their grandchildren and were worried sick about what would happen to them if the dragons continued on the path they'd set.

They loved Ollis, too, of course. He was their son, and not having children wouldn't change that. But, like Malcolm, they thought that he didn't have kids because he wasn't serious about his future. They believed he just wanted to have fun and not deal with anything serious, and he didn't know how to make them see that wasn't the case.

He'd grown up. He wasn't a teenager anymore. He was almost thirty, and while he wasn't married, that didn't mean he wasn't an adult. What if he never found someone he could imagine spending the rest of his life with? Why would it make him less than Malcolm?

Telling his parents and his brother this wouldn't change anything. They saw Ollis as a teenager who wasn't serious about anything, and Ollis wasn't sure there was anything he could do to change that. He'd stopped trying a few years back, and it had been a relief, but he still got angry sometimes.

"I mean, do you even have someone right now?" Malcolm continued, clearly oblivious to the fact that Ollis hadn't been listening to him. "When was the last time you had a serious relationship? Have you thought about it?"

Ollis could tell that if he stayed, he was going to say something he'd regret or worse, *do* something he'd regret, like punching his brother.

Actually, that didn't sound like something he'd regret. Maybe he should do that.

He shook his head and got to his feet. Hitting Malcolm would make him feel better, but that would only last for a few seconds. After it was over, he'd have to deal with the mess left behind, and that wasn't something he was willing to do.

"Just because I didn't marry the first person who could stand me longer than half an hour doesn't mean I'm not a good person," he told his brother. "If I ever get married, I want it to be to someone I can see myself spending the rest of my life with, not to the person I gave my first kiss to. Maybe you're the one who has to do some growing up. It looks like you're stuck in your teenage years, and that can't be good."

Malcolm spluttered while their mother tried to stop Ollis from leaving.

He loved his family, even Malcolm, but they got on his nerves. For some reason, they'd always believed he wasn't serious about anything in life. He had a job and his own place, but it still wasn't enough. He suspected it would never be until he did what Malcolm had done and gave his parents grandkids.

But what if Ollis didn't want kids? He loved Malcolm's children but couldn't see himself having his own children, and he didn't think that would ever change. Considering the situation the pack was in, it certainly wasn't going to change anytime soon. There was no way to know how the pack would survive the fight with dragons or if it would at all.

Ollis put on his shoes in the entrance and ignored his mother calling for him. He was terrified at the thought of anything happening to her or the rest of his family, and he wasn't the only one. Everyone in the pack was tense and on edge. The dragons were messing everything up, and Ollis hated them for it. He wanted them to pay, but he was only one wolf shifter.

Luckily, he wasn't the one making decisions. He supposed he could have dealt easily enough with everyday situations, but finding allies to fight a dragon clan was out of his depth. He hoped that wasn't the case for Kieran. If they wanted to win this war, they needed fighters, and for now, the ones they had weren't enough. The dragons were stronger, and that wasn't even considering the fact that they could shift into dragons. Their clan was powerful and rich, and they were terrorizing the city. Everyone was terrified at the thought of them attacking again, and it was a legitimate fear.

These dragon shifters didn't care about peace or the fact that people just wanted to live their lives. They only cared about themselves and their power, and attacking the mall had showed everyone just how much of it they had.

Enough to eradicate the pack from existence.

"Are you sure you'll be fine here on your own?" Meyer asked his brother.

Parker waved him off. "It's not like he's going to open the

door and come out. I'll be fine. Go get something to eat, and maybe bring me a snack."

After the conversation they'd had about Luca, Meyer was a bit wary of leaving Parker alone with him, but he didn't believe that Parker would let Luca out. He might try to get answers out of him, but he wasn't stupid. No matter how attracted he was to Luca or how he thought Luca wouldn't betray them, he wouldn't jeopardize his family and the pack by doing something stupid.

That was why Meyer felt good enough to leave him behind. He made his way down the stairs and to the kitchen, opening the fridge to find out that someone had drunk the last of the blood. He groaned and swore that if he got his hands on whoever it had been, he'd strangle them.

"Great," he muttered. "Now I have to go out and buy blood."

Luckily, he knew where to go. When he and his family had arrived in town, one of the first things they'd done was check if there were other vampires in the area and how they got their blood. It had been fairly easy to find, and Meyer now knew that if he went to a specific service station, the owner would give him what he needed. The man was human, but his partner wasn't. Apparently, he'd started stocking and selling blood after meeting her, and it had become a business. Meyer was glad for that. The last thing he wanted was to have to hunt his dinner in the situation the pack was in.

He headed out and reached the service station after a short drive. He got enough blood for himself and his family for a few days and made a mental note to tell Tyrian to send someone else to refill. Usually, they kept an eye on the fridge so they didn't run low, but everything was a mess these days, so Meyer wasn't surprised that no one had realized it was almost empty.

Meyer felt better by the time he was back in the car driving toward pack territory again. His stomach was full, and he felt stronger, but also like he wouldn't say no to a nap.

Something in the forest caught his eye. That happened often these days. Meyer wasn't used to living with a bunch of wolves, but it made sense that they used the forest where they lived to stretch their legs, both in their human and wolf form. It was probably nothing, but just in case, he decided to check. With part of the pack having left to follow Kieran's sister, it would be good to make sure that the wolf running around was a pack member.

Meyer parked the car on the side of the road and hesitated. Should he go out and confront the wolf? Would they even answer if he asked them who they were? Even if they belonged to the pack, they didn't have to. Technically, Meyer was no one. He certainly wasn't the alpha, and no one owed him any kind of explanation.

He reminded himself that this wolf could belong to Fay, and if so, everyone needed to know.

He left the car as soon as he parked and moved in the direction from which the wolf was coming. He waited for the wolf to reach him, knowing the instant the wolf noticed him.

They stopped running. They didn't shift right away, but they stared at Meyer. The wolf was panting, and the way their tongue lolled to the side was adorable. Meyer was pretty sure that if he mentioned it, the wolf would try to tear his head off, so he didn't.

"Sorry to bother you," he said. "I'm sure you can understand that I wanted to check who you are and if you belong with the pack."

Meyer didn't expect much from the wolf. Some pack members were still wary of him and his family, which he understood. They weren't used to sharing their living spaces with vampires, and while they'd had to learn after their alpha had fallen in love with a vamp, it didn't mean they were happy about having a bunch of vampires in their territory. Meyer wouldn't be in their place.

To his surprise, the wolf shifted. He averted his gaze, not for the first time wondering how the wolves could be so comfortable being naked around other people. He understood it was something they got used to as kids, but still. Wasn't the wolf cold? Spring had just started, but it was still too cold to walk around naked.

"You don't have to worry. I'm a member of this pack, and I'd rather die than follow Fay," the wolf said.

Meyer thought he'd recognized his voice, so he peeked at the wolf's face. He relaxed when he saw that he was right and that he did know the wolf.

Ollis wasn't a traitor. Meyer didn't know him well, but he'd heard enough from him and about him to be sure of that.

Ollis grinned. "Still not used to living with shifters?"

Meyer shook his head. "I don't get the nudity thing."

"That's probably because you're old."

Meyer barked out a laugh. He hadn't expected Ollis to tease him, and he was delighted. It was good to see that at least some of the wolves treated him and the other vampires like pack members and as if they weren't any different from the wolves.

"I *am* old," Meyer confirmed. "But I believe I wear my age well."

"I guess you are pretty sexy for an old guy."

Meyer blinked. He didn't think Ollis was trying to seduce him, but he was definitely flirting. That was a surprise, too. No matter how comfortable Ollis seemed to be, Meyer hadn't expected that. "Well, my age means I've had a lot of time to learn things."

Ollis's smile widened. "What kind of things?"

Meyer had no idea where this was going, but he was enjoying himself. He could see goosebumps on Ollis's skin, though. Ollis shouldn't be standing out here. "Why don't you get into my car? I'll drive you back."

"Is this you trying to have your way with me? Because it might just work."

Meyer laughed again. "Not really, but I can make an effort if it'll convince you to say yes."

Ollis shivered. "Oh, you don't have to convince me. It's probably better if I shift back, though. I don't think you want my naked ass on your car seat."

Meyer wasn't sure about that, but he quickly opened the trunk of his car and took out one of the blankets he kept there. "Here. This way, you won't have to sit your naked ass on my car seat, but we'll be able to have a conversation."

Ollis looked surprised but took the blanket. "Thank you."

"You're welcome," Meyer said with a smile.

The blanket was big enough to wrap all the way around Ollis. It covered him from his shoulders to his knees, and while he'd still be slightly cold, at least he wasn't completely naked anymore.

Ollis rubbed his cheek against the blanket. "It's soft."

"Thank you."

"What do you mean? Don't tell me you made this."

Meyer waited until they were in the car to answer. "I did. Being a vampire and having eternity to learn things means that sometimes you get bored and learn to crochet, then you crochet for weeks at a time while barely stopping to do anything else, including feeding."

"But this is massive," Ollis commented as he looked down. "And it's beautiful. I like the colors."

Meyer was a muted colors kind of guy. The colors he'd chosen for this blanket were all variations of gray and green. Ollis liked it, and Meyer felt stupidly happy about that.

Something was happening here, and while he had no idea what that something was, he was eager to find out.

Ollis was stunned. He'd always associated knitting and all of that stuff with older ladies like his mother. She made him and everyone else in the family knit sweaters for Christmas, and she was pretty good at it. Ollis loved those sweaters, and he wore them all the time.

He hadn't expected a vampire to do the same kind of thing. He had no idea how old Meyer was, but what he'd said about having too much time made sense. Ollis couldn't imagine being a vampire. What was it like to have infinite time to learn whatever you wanted to learn?

It had to get boring after a while, which would explain why Meyer had taken up crocheting. The blanket was soft and big enough to cover Ollis and all of his bits, and it felt lovely after standing in the cold.

Ollis had been surprised when Meyer had stopped him. He hadn't thought Meyer would do anything to hurt him. Meyer was a pack member, and several of his family members were dating wolves. It *had* been a bit of a surprise to realize that Meyer cared about the pack enough to feel like he needed to check on intruders. It was endearing and added to Meyer's charm, which he didn't need.

Ollis already found Meyer sexy enough as it was.

He tried to think about his brother's reaction if Ollis told him he was dating a vampire. Even though he'd been telling Ollis to find a partner for years, Malcolm would pitch a fit. He wanted Ollis to find himself a nice wolf, preferably a woman.

As if Ollis hadn't told everyone in his family he was gay when he was fourteen.

He'd been lucky. His parents had accepted it, and while they'd told him to keep it a secret for as long as he could, he'd known it wasn't because they were ashamed of him. Kieran's father was the alpha back then, and it would have been dangerous for Ollis to be out.

It wasn't anymore. Kieran was the alpha now, and he had a male partner. Robin was even a vampire, and Ollis couldn't help but wonder which part of that had scandalized Kieran's father the most. Was it that Robin was a guy or that he was a vampire? There was no way to know since Ollis wasn't about to find the old alpha to ask, but it amused him.

Just like the thought of introducing Meyer to Malcolm as his boyfriend amused him. Their parents would probably take it in stride, but not Malcolm. Even if he could get over Meyer being a vampire, he wouldn't waste any time pointing out that neither Ollis nor Meyer could have kids. He didn't understand that not everyone wanted children, and sometimes, Ollis hated him for that.

What was it about being a parent that made some people feel superior? As far as Ollis was concerned, having kids was just a sign that people had unprotected sex, and it wasn't something he wanted to think about when it came to his brother.

Ollis stroked his hand down the blanket. "My grandmother used to crochet," he said. "My mom does, too, but she mostly knits."

"You never learned?"

Ollis shook his head. "I tried, but my fingers can't seem to do it." He hesitated. "I guess I'm too clumsy."

"Maybe, or maybe you didn't give it enough time."

"I don't think I'd have the patience to do anything like this, anyway. It had to have taken you a long time."

Meyer flashed Ollis a smile. "It did, but I have nothing but time."

Because he was a vampire. Maybe Ollis should feel afraid or wary, but he didn't. Every vampire he'd met from Meyer's family was lovely, and he'd trust them sooner than he'd trust some of the pack members. After all, a bunch of them had betrayed Kieran and followed his sister away from the pack. Those wolves wouldn't hesitate to stab Ollis in the back, but Meyer and his family wouldn't. That made them better pack members than the ones who'd left.

"You should keep it," Meyer said.

Ollis frowned. "The blanket?"

"I have plenty of time to make more."

"I don't want to take it away from you. It's too beautiful."

"I have a lot of blankets at home, Ollis. Giving you this one isn't going to change that or the fact that I'm working on two more blankets at the moment. I've run out of people willing to accept my crochet gifts. It would be a pleasure for me if you took this one."

Ollis's instinct was telling him to say no, but he found himself nodding anyway. He *wanted* to keep the blanket, and not just because it was soft. Clearly this was important to Meyer, and for some reason, Ollis wanted to make Meyer happy. "Well, thank you," he said.

"You're welcome. I'm glad I found someone who appreciates my work. My siblings are used to it by now, but I've made a bunch of stuff for every one of them, and they have enough."

Ollis hadn't run far out in pack territory, so they were already almost home. He didn't want his time with Meyer to end, but he wasn't sure there was anything he could do to make it last longer. Maybe he could strike up another conversation. "How's that dragon doing?"

Meyer glanced at him. "You mean Luca?"

"The new one."

Ollis had been present when the mall had been attacked. He still had nightmares about some of the things he'd seen that day, and it was easier for him to focus on the people who'd survived. He was also curious to find out what the dragon was doing here. He'd heard Luca wanted to help the pack, but he wasn't sure anyone could trust him. Kieran certainly didn't. He and the vampires kept Luca locked up in a bedroom in the house where the vampires lived, and Ollis couldn't help but wonder how long they'd keep him there. Maybe until the fight with the clan was over. At the very least, it would mean the clan was one dragon down.

But they really needed more help, especially from other dragons. The pack had two, but it wouldn't be enough against an entire clan.

This might not be Ollis's problem to solve, but he was as involved as anyone else in the pack. If something happened to Kieran or if the dragons attacked the pack, he and his family would suffer. He didn't want to consider it, but what could he do?

"Luca seems to be fine," Meyer answered. "He still insists he wants to help."

"You believe him?"

Meyer took a moment to answer. "I do. I don't think he's here to spy on us or hurt us. I don't believe the clan needs to spy on us. They could take us down at any moment if they wish to do so. The pack doesn't have anything they want. They just want us out of the way."

"Why would he have left them?"

"Maybe because he felt it was the right thing to do. You didn't go with Fay when she left."

Ollis could see where Meyer was going. "Because it wouldn't have been right. She wouldn't have been a good alpha."

Ollis, Fay, Kieran, and a bunch of others had grown up together. Ollis wouldn't say that Fay had been his best friend, but he'd known her as a child and teenager. Her father had spoiled her, and she'd be too selfish as an alpha. The fact that she'd allied with the dragons was the perfect example of that. She was throwing a tantrum because Kieran had taken the pack from her, and she was ready to destroy anyone who'd stayed behind. She didn't have the pack's best interest at heart, only hers.

"We need more allies," he murmured.

"We do," Meyer agreed. "Kieran's working on it. Everyone is."

They could only hope they'd find enough people by the time the clan finally attacked.

It was only a matter of time before they did.

Chapter Two

"Who's out there? Parker?"

Meyer groaned at the sound of Luca's voice. Luca expected Parker to be here, which meant Parker had talked to him. They hadn't been forbidden to do so, but it took Parker one step closer to becoming the disaster Meyer was afraid was brewing. If his brother was getting to know Luca, it meant they were growing closer, and that way lay trouble.

"Not Parker," Luca murmured.

It would be better if Meyer stayed quiet, but he was curious, and there wasn't much to do while he sat next to the bedroom door. "Not Parker," he confirmed. "I'm Meyer."

For a moment, Luca was silent. Meyer wondered if he'd decided not to speak since Parker wasn't here. He wouldn't mind either way. Actually, it would probably be better if he stopped talking to Luca.

"You're one of Parker's brothers."

Parker had *definitely* talked to Luca before. "I am. How many conversations have you had with Parker?"

"Not enough. I understand I'm a prisoner, but it doesn't mean I have to be stuck alone in this bedroom."

Meyer thought that was the description of being a prisoner, but he didn't say it. "What have you and my brother talked about?"

"Not the clan."

"Why not? Don't you want to give us information about them?"

"Would you believe what I tell you, or would you think I

was trying to betray you?"

"Can you betray us if you're not one of us?" It was harsh, but Meyer wanted Luca to answer. Why was he here? Was it really to help, or was there something more to it?

Luca wouldn't answer. If he was a spy, it would give him up, and if he wasn't, he didn't have a reason to. If he wasn't a spy, the pack hadn't been treating him well, so why would he want to help? If he wasn't a spy, he'd left his life and everyone who mattered to him to help the clan, and the pack had locked him up.

"I might not be one of you, but it doesn't mean I want the clan to take over the area," Luca said in a quiet voice. "You've only just started dealing with the clan, so you don't know the extent of what they're ready to do. They're power-hungry and bloodthirsty. The town didn't matter to them before, but the alpha holds grudges. Your alpha went against him, and he didn't like that."

"Kieran had to do something to protect his people. It's not like he wants control of the area, so I don't get it."

"He might not want control of the area, but he also doesn't want the dragons to have it, and he certainly doesn't want them to hurt the people who live here. He and his friends have warned the supernatural communities about the clan and their drugs, and my alpha had specific plans that involved it. You thwarted that plan."

Meyer hadn't been there when all of this had happened, but he'd been told about it. From what he remembered, the dragons had spread the drugs in an attempt to kill as many supernatural creatures as they could, possibly to take over the area. They'd thought the various groups would blame each other, and they had, but thankfully, it hadn't lasted long.

"Is that why you left? Because you wanted nothing to do with the takeover?" Meyer asked.

"I was never comfortable with anything the alpha does. I

don't want to be a criminal. I want to find happiness and be allowed to live it the way I want. I always knew it wouldn't be possible if I stayed."

"So you left."

"I should have left sooner, but I'm not as brave as Merrick and Arlen. They were trailblazers. They showed the rest of us that it could be done, and I know several people who had plans to follow the lead."

"Had?"

"Everyone knows what the clan did to the club Merrick and Arlen own. They're afraid, and I don't think they're wrong to be."

Meyer agreed with that. He was aware of Merrick and Arlen's story. They'd left the clan and had been left alone for a long time. They'd built their club and had made it successful. The clan had left them alone until they'd gotten closer to the pack. When they had, the clan had burned the club to the ground.

Meyer could have blamed the people who were stuck with the clan, but he saw it for what it was. The alpha was abusive, and most of the people there didn't have anywhere else to go. Merrick and Arlen had explained a bit about how the clan worked, so Meyer knew that every bit of money a dragon earned through their job went to the clan. The dragons all lived in the same house under the alpha's thumb. Unless they had someone outside of the clan, they wouldn't have anywhere to go or any kind of resource if they left. The only thing they would have was the clan hunting them, and if they had kids or family, it would be unthinkable to put them through that. Arlen and Merrick had been on their own, and Meyer suspected that Luca was, too. What about everyone else, though? What about the families?

"How many followers does your alpha have?" he asked.

"Now you're asking the right questions. He doesn't have

as many supporters as he thinks, but you still need more people. The pack won't be able to do anything on their own."

Meyer tapped his fingertips on his thigh. "We need big shifters and people who can hold their own against a dragon."

"You need more dragons."

Meyer grinned. "What about hydras?"

Meyer had been poking around on his phone before Luca interrupted him, so he was quick to find the number he was looking for. Luca was still talking, but Meyer had something better to focus on.

He couldn't believe he hadn't thought of this sooner. It might not help, so maybe it would be better if he didn't mention it to anyone yet, but it might also give them a chance.

"To what do I owe the pleasure?" Alice asked when she answered. "It's been a while since I last heard from you, Meyer. I might have thought you'd died, except you're a vampire."

"I haven't died," Meyer promised.

"I would have been worried if you had and were still calling me," Alice said with a laugh. "It's good to hear from you. What are you up to?"

"I need help." Meyer might as well get straight to the point.

"Would you believe me if I told you I knew you'd say that? You only call me when you need something."

"I'm sorry, Alice, but this is serious. I'll make it up to you once everyone's safe."

Her tone became more serious. "Tell me."

"Several members of my family have recently found partners, and they all belong to a wolf pack. There's a dragon clan in the area, and they've been trying to take control, but the pack is standing in their way. It's a mess, Alice. We need allies."

"Shit. This is more serious than I expected. I've heard about this, Meyer, and it's not good. Everyone expects the dragons to win."

Meyer wasn't surprised. He'd noticed the many supernatural creatures leaving the area. They didn't want to stay and answer to the clan, so they ran.

But the pack couldn't run. This was their home, and they belonged here. Even if running was an option, many of the wolves wouldn't even think about it.

"Do you think you can help?" Meyer asked.

Alice hesitated. "Honestly? Our clan is torn. Some of us think we should step in because if we don't, the dragons will keep attacking people and trying to expand. We might not be close by, but eventually, they might reach us, and if they do, we'll need allies. Others believe we should stay out of it. They feel it's not our business."

"What does your sister think?" Alice's sister, Carla, was the alpha of their clan of hydras. She'd be the one making the final decision.

"She hasn't decided yet. I didn't know you were involved, so I stayed out of it."

Meyer closed his eyes. He and Alice were friends, and while they talked often enough on the phone, they hadn't seen each other in a few years. Meyer wouldn't be surprised if Alice chose her clan over him. In fact, he expected her to.

"I'll talk to her," Alice said. "I can't make any promises, though."

"That's all I was hoping for. Thank you, Alice."

"Don't thank me yet. You don't know what she'll say."

"I don't, but you're giving me more hope than I've had in a while. Even if she says no, at least I tried."

It might not be enough, but it was something to cling to.

Ollis resisted the urge to take out his phone and check the message he'd gotten earlier for what would have to be the hundredth time.

Why did Sloan and Kieran want to see him?

He hadn't done anything that would make his alpha want to yell at him, or at least, he didn't think so. He'd stayed out of trouble and had focused on his work and keeping his pack safe. He'd been patrolling the area when Kieran asked him to, going to work, and that was it.

None of that would warrant a visit to the alpha. There had to be something more, but Ollis couldn't think of anything, and he'd been torturing himself since he got the text this morning.

Thankfully, the wait was over. He'd reached Kieran's house, and Kieran was waiting for him inside. He'd tell Ollis what was up, and Ollis could find a way to make things right if they were wrong.

What the fuck had he gotten himself into?

He knocked on the door and quickly sucked in a breath. He couldn't faint in front of his alpha. He hadn't done anything wrong, and Kieran was a fair alpha. He wouldn't accuse Ollis of doing things he hadn't done the way his father might have.

The door swung open. Ollis had expected Kieran's partner, Robin, to open, but it was Sloan. The beta was Kieran's brother, and he'd resisted becoming his brother's beta. Kieran had chosen well, though. With him and Sloan at the lead, the pack was safe.

As long as the dragons didn't attack them, anyway.

Sloan smiled. "Hi."

"Please tell me I'm not in trouble," Ollis blurted out.

Sloan blinked, then shook his head. "You're not. Is that what you thought?"

"When your beta texts you that your alpha wants to talk to you, of course you're going to assume you're in trouble. It wouldn't be the first time."

Ollis had gotten in trouble before, but that was over. He'd

grown up and had his life in hand, and he needed Sloan and Kieran to realize that.

"Well, you're not in trouble, so don't worry."

"Has something happened, then?"

"Why don't you come in? Kieran wants to tell you himself."

So there *was* something. What was it? No matter how hard Ollis focused, he just couldn't think of anything.

He followed Sloan inside the house. He left his jacket and his boots in the entrance, then headed toward Kieran's office.

He knew the place well. He hadn't been here often since Kieran had become the alpha, but he'd visited almost weekly when his father was. There was always something the old alpha was angry about, and he'd scolded Ollis more than Ollis's parents ever had.

Ollis realized he'd been lucky. It could have ended badly if Kieran's father had decided to make an example out of him. No one would have been able to stop him, not even Ollis's family.

Kieran was behind his desk. He looked up when he heard Sloan and Ollis, and his smile was genuine as he gestured to Ollis to sit down on the other side of his desk.

"He thought he was in trouble," Sloan announced.

"What did you tell him?" Kieran asked his brother.

Sloan shrugged. "That we wanted to talk to him."

Kieran waited, then laughed. "That's it?"

"What else was I supposed to tell him?"

"Maybe not to worry because it was nothing bad?" Kieran looked at Ollis. "Sorry about that. Sloan's a good beta, but he could be more diplomatic."

"It's fine. I just really want to know what's going on."

Sloan sat down, and the brothers looked at Ollis for a moment. Ollis told himself that everything was all right, but he was still nervous, so he bounced his knee up and down, hoping it wouldn't bother them.

"Things with the dragons have been going from bad to worse," Kieran eventually said. "I don't have to tell you that. You were there to see the aftermath of what they did at the mall."

Ollis briefly closed his eyes. "I was."

"I'm sorry you had to go through that, but I'm thankful for your help, and I know I'm not the only one. But as you know, the dragons are coming for us, and we need to find allies. We won't be able to stand up to them as it is, unfortunately. Even if the pack were stronger, I doubt we'd be able to win against a clan of dragons."

Ollis could imagine a dragon and a wolf fighting, and it wasn't pretty. Maybe if they had numbers on their side, they could win, but they didn't, and even worse, most of the pack members were normal people with families and jobs. They weren't fighters.

"Sloan and I have to focus on finding these allies, but unfortunately, it leaves us very little time to take care of the everyday problems in the pack. That's where you come in."

Ollis frowned. "What do you mean?"

"We've been watching you. You had the reputation of a troublemaker before, but you've grown. You've become more responsible, and it's good to see," Sloan said. "We need someone we can trust to be alpha in the interim, and we both agree that person is you."

Ollis tried making sense of what Sloan was saying, but his brain couldn't. "What does that mean?"

"Sloan and I have to focus on the dragons," Kieran interjected. "We need to meet potential allies. I wish we could do all of that on the phone or the computer, but many of these people want to meet us face-to-face. They want to be sure we're not like the dragons and that they wouldn't help us win, only for us to turn around and be even worse than the clan.

We're hoping we'll be able to convince several community leaders to help, but doing so will take a lot of time and energy. Neither of us can focus on the pack while we do this, which is where we're hoping you can come in. We'll make a public announcement and explain to the pack that until the war is over, you'll be in charge of everyday life. If they have a problem or complaints, they should come to you. You'll have the authority to solve these problems as you see fit. We'll always be available if you need to talk things out, of course, but we both agree that we trust you enough that we don't expect you to contact us before making decisions."

Ollis gaped. He could try to speak, but he doubted anything intelligent would come out of his mouth.

How had Sloan and Kieran decided he was the best person to do this? He could think of a dozen who would be better. "What about Robin? He's the alpha mate, so he should be the one doing this, right? Not that he has to if he doesn't want to," Ollis quickly added. It wouldn't be great to badmouth the alpha mate.

"We considered it, but he and I haven't been together long, and some pack members are still uncomfortable with him. It's understandable, but right now, it's a problem. Having you in charge will make everyone comfortable, and in the end, that's what we want. Robin will help you as much as you need, but he didn't grow up in a pack, so he doesn't know how it works well enough. I think that the two of you together will be a formidable team."

"I'm still not sure why you chose me."

Kieran's expression softened. "Because we trust you. After what happened with Fay, it wasn't easy to choose someone both Sloan and I trust. There's always a part of us that wonders if whoever we choose is going to betray us, maybe take over the pack, or hand it over to Fay."

"But you don't think I will?"

"No. You'll keep the pack safe and be ready to hand it back over as soon as the war is over."

Kieran was right. Ollis had never thought about being the alpha. Hell, he'd been happy he wasn't in charge because he didn't think he would have known how to deal with the challenges Kieran was dealing with. He would never want to be the alpha for longer than he strictly had to, and even then, he wasn't comfortable being called alpha.

"You'll have to tell me what to do," he warned.

Kieran grinned. "We will. As long as you say yes, we can work with that."

There was no way Ollis would say no. He might not want to do it, but his alpha was asking, and there was only one acceptable answer. "I'll do it."

"You can go," Parker declared as he flopped into the second chair in the hallway.

Meyer stared at him. After he'd ended his conversation with Alice, he and Luca hadn't talked again. Meyer had been glad because it gave him time to think and, more importantly, time to text a few more people. He should have done so before, but he wasn't used to relying on people or asking for favors. He only did that with his family, and they were already deep in this. What they needed was more people, people dragons wouldn't expect, like Alice and her hydras.

Meyer didn't have answers yet, but he'd get them eventually. He'd already decided he wouldn't tell anyone he'd reached out in case he got bad news. He hoped Luca wouldn't tell anyone, but even if he did, it wouldn't hurt anyone as long as they were cautious with their hope.

"Earth to Meyer," Parker said, reaching forward with his foot and poking Meyer's leg. "What happened?"

Meyer shook his head. "Nothing. Your boyfriend was

perfectly nice."

Parker narrowed his eyes. "He's not my boyfriend."

"Yet."

Parker glanced at the bedroom door, but neither of them could hear anything. Maybe Luca wasn't listening to them, or maybe he was and wanted to talk to Parker. It was none of Meyer's business. He'd already warned Parker to be careful, so the ball was in Parker's court.

"Seriously," Parker said. "What happened?"

"Nothing important. Luca was fine. We had a conversation about his clan and what he thinks it's going to take to get the dragons to stop coming after the pack. It wasn't the nicest chat, but that had nothing to do with Luca and everything to do with his clan."

"He's helpless."

"He's worried, but then, we all are."

Meyer's phone vibrated in his hand, and he quickly looked at the screen. He'd hoped Alice would already have an answer, but he wasn't surprised to see it wasn't her. It would take time to know what the hydras would do. Alice would have to talk to her sister first, and Carla would speak with her advisors and possibly the rest of her clan. She'd need time to make her decision.

Meyer was afraid they might not have enough of it.

Ollis had texted him, and he quickly opened the message. He frowned when he saw that Ollis wanted to talk to him. Had something happened?

"You can go," Parker said, gently pushing Meyer's leg again. "I'll stay here with Luca."

Meyer didn't hesitate to get to his feet. "Stay away from him," he warned.

"Of course."

Meyer narrowed his eyes. "I know you. You say one thing, then do the exact opposite. I can't stop you from deciding to be with Luca, but please be careful."

"Sounds to me like you *are* trying to stop me," Parker grumbled.

He was right, but Meyer didn't have time to deal with his brother right now. Trying to talk some sense into Parker was intense, but Ollis needed Meyer.

Meyer didn't understand why. He was sure Ollis had plenty of friends to talk to, yet he wanted to talk to Meyer. Why? What had happened that he needed to talk to a vampire?

Luckily, Meyer wouldn't have to go far to find out. Ollis had mentioned that he was in the woods outside the house, and Meyer saw him as soon as he stepped out the door.

Ollis was at the edge of the trees, pacing back and forth and apparently talking to himself. Meyer took a moment to watch him.

No adult man was supposed to be adorable, but it was the first word that came to mind when Meyer looked at Ollis. Besides, Ollis wasn't the only man Meyer found adorable. Alpin could be called that, although considering his personality, anyone who actually believed he was adorable was in for a rude awakening.

But unlike Alpin, Ollis was sweet. He was also troubled, which only partially explained why he wanted to talk to Meyer.

"Ollis?" Meyer called out as he moved forward.

Ollis looked up. He was frowning, a sure sign something was wrong. "Did I bother you?"

Meyer wasn't sure where they stood, but he was sure that whatever Ollis did, he could never bother him. "No, of course not. What happened?"

"I got a text from Sloan that he and Kieran wanted to talk to me."

Meyer couldn't think of any reason for the alpha to be

angry at Ollis, but it wasn't like he and Ollis spent a lot of time together. They'd exchanged phone numbers after Meyer had given Ollis a ride the other day, and they'd texted a few times, but that was it, so naturally he'd been surprised when Ollis asked to see him.

Ollis stopped in front of Meyer. "They wanted to talk about how they're going to have a lot of meetings in the near future, and they both might have to leave pack territory to meet these people, and how even when they're here, they can't focus on the everyday problems of the pack. Usually, the alpha mate would be the person the pack goes to, but considering Robin's a vampire and only recently moved in, both Sloan and Kieran thought it would be better to ask someone else to be in charge."

Meyer had a hard time following. He understood what Ollis was saying. It made sense that even though that was supposed to be Robin's job, he couldn't do it. Not only was he a vampire in a pack full of wolf shifters, but he also hadn't grown up in a pack. He wouldn't know what his role was supposed to be or how to behave, so having Kieran choose someone else was understandable.

"They asked me to do it," Ollis continued.

Meyer hadn't expected that, and from the look of it, neither had Ollis. "How do you feel about that?"

"I don't know. I know I should be happy, and part of me is. I can't believe both Sloan and Kieran trust me enough to want me to be in charge when they can't be. I just don't understand why me. Even though Robin isn't the best choice, there has to be someone better, right?"

"Clearly not. They wouldn't have asked you if they'd had anyone better in mind. Don't you want to do it?" Being in charge of the pack was a lot of responsibilities, even though Ollis wouldn't actually be the alpha.

"I want to make them proud and show them they chose the

right person, but at the same time, I don't know if I can do it. I can't even get my brother to stop bothering me about having kids and growing up. How am I supposed to deal with the entire pack?"

Ollis moved, maybe to start pacing again, but Meyer stopped him with a hand on his arm. Ollis turned wide eyes to him, and Meyer could see the panic lurking there. "Take a deep breath," he ordered.

To his surprise, Ollis obeyed without hesitation. He sucked in a breath, then another when Meyer didn't say anything.

Meyer wasn't sure how long they stayed there, but eventually, Ollis calmed down. He still looked bewildered, but Meyer didn't expect that to change anytime soon. "Did you tell them you'd do it?" he asked.

"Yeah. I probably should have asked for time to think, but I couldn't say no."

"Did you *want* to say yes? Because I'm sure they'll both accept it if you go back and tell them you decided you weren't up for it."

Ollis squared his shoulders and straightened his back. "I'm not going to change my mind. I told them I'd do it, and I will."

Meyer grinned. "Good. I'm convinced you'll be great at it. Besides, you're not doing this alone."

"Robin will help me as much as he can, and Kieran and Sloan already told me that I could contact them if I needed anything."

Meyer had meant that *he* was willing to help Ollis if he needed anything, but this was good, too. "See? Even if there's something you don't know how to do or if someone gives you trouble, you won't have to deal with it on your own. They'll help you. It's a lot of responsibility, but you can do it."

Meyer truly believed that. Now, he needed Ollis to feel the same.

Ollis wanted to believe Meyer. He wanted to believe that he was good enough to do this and that he could earn the pack's respect, but what if he couldn't? What if they believed that Ollis was just a kid and that he shouldn't be put in charge?

What if they decided not to do what he asked when he gave an order?

It wouldn't be his fault, and he had no doubt that if he explained it to Kieran, the alpha would be pissed with the pack and not Ollis, but still. It would show him that Ollis couldn't do this, and Ollis was afraid he'd lose Kieran's respect.

He wished he could get his hands on his old self and throttle him. What had he been thinking, behaving like a teenager even when he was in his twenties?

To be fair, he'd been in his early twenties and had been rebelling against Kieran's father. He'd straightened up quickly once Kieran had taken his father's place, but he had a reputation.

It wasn't even well-earned. He *had* created some trouble, but it hadn't been anything bad. Mostly, it had been disobeying the alpha's orders, but that alpha wasn't Kieran, and Kieran knew how bad his father had been. Surely, he wouldn't hold that against Ollis.

He *wasn't* holding it against him. He'd given Ollis a job that would make him responsible for the pack. Ollis would never have believed something like this could happen, and he didn't know what he'd do if he failed.

It looked like even though people had faith in him, he didn't have faith in himself, and he didn't know how to deal with that.

Ollis straightened his back and raised his chin. "I can do it," he said, trying to convince himself.

Meyer smiled. "You can. Besides, Kieran, Sloan, and Robin won't be the only people helping you."

Ollis snorted. "I can't imagine my family will. My brother thinks I'm useless."

Meyer chuckled. "He's not who I meant. *I'll* help you as much as I can, as will the rest of my family. We might not know a lot about wolf packs, but it doesn't mean we're useless. My father especially could be of use."

Ollis hadn't expected that. He liked Meyer and was glad Meyer had come running when he'd asked to meet him, but that didn't mean Meyer was going to be there for him.

Why would he? They barely knew each other, and they were so different. Meyer was a vampire. He'd lived decades longer than Ollis, and Ollis could only imagine everything he'd seen during those decades. Ollis had never left the area around pack territory and wasn't planning to. This was his home, and he didn't want to travel. He was fine staying here, especially now that Kieran was in charge.

How could that interest Meyer? Ollis had no idea, but Meyer was offering his help, and Ollis wasn't about to say no. He didn't know how the pack would react to him being in charge, but it felt good to know that Meyer and his family were on his side, whatever happened.

Ollis nodded. "Thank you."

"You're welcome. I'm sorry you panicked, but I hope I managed to make you feel better about it. You'll do a splendid job, but you have to relax. Being frantic won't help."

"You sound like you've been through this before."

Meyer grinned, exposing his fangs. Before meeting vampires, Ollis had wondered how he'd feel if he did. He'd expected to be afraid, but he wasn't, especially not of Meyer. Meyer had only ever been nice to him, supporting him when even Ollis's family wouldn't. Ollis could imagine what would have happened if he'd asked to see his brother tonight. Malcolm would have laughed in his face, and he'd have been sure that Kieran and Sloan had made a mistake.

But not Meyer. He'd told Ollis he had faith in him, and he wasn't lying. Maybe Ollis's family wasn't that important after all. Maybe what they thought of him didn't actually matter.

"I have," Meyer said. "As you like to remind me, I'm old. People either have too much self-esteem or not enough. You just needed someone to give you a little push, and I was happy to do so."

What was Ollis supposed to do with this man? Meyer was looking at him with a fond expression that made Ollis want to kiss him. This would probably be the stupidest thing he could do, but why not?

Kieran was dating a vampire. Sloan was, too. Why couldn't Ollis?

He decided to be brave like Meyer thought he was. He leaned forward, hoping Meyer wouldn't jump away in disgust, and pressed their lips together. He wanted more but was terrified that Meyer didn't see him that way. He wouldn't be surprised. After all, he was a young wolf shifter, while Meyer was a very old vampire who'd seen the world.

"What was that for?" Meyer asked in a soft voice.

Ollis told himself that didn't mean Meyer hadn't wanted it. He just wanted an explanation. "I like you," he said honestly. His heart raced, but there was no way out of it. "You believe in me in a way that even my family doesn't. I don't think anyone has ever believed in me like that, not even me. You make me *want* to be brave and strong, and no one's ever made me feel that way. I'm sorry if I did something you didn't want."

Meyer reached for Ollis, and for a moment, Ollis wondered if he was going to hit him. Other men would have.

But not Meyer. Instead, he pulled Ollis into his arms, cradling him against his chest. When Ollis looked up, Meyer kissed him, and this time, it was much more than just a press of the lips.

Ollis opened his mouth, welcoming Meyer in. Meyer's

tongue invaded his mouth, and Ollis groaned as he tried to push closer. Meyer's arms were like bands of steel around him, holding him in place and keeping him safe at the same time.

Ollis was going to need all of this. He was sure he could do a good job and make Kieran and Sloan proud, but he'd need help.

Thankfully, he'd have it.

He was curious about Meyer's fangs, so he gently prodded at one with the tip of his tongue. Meyer groaned, surprising Ollis. Ollis didn't particularly enjoy using teeth in bed or while he kissed, but maybe things were different for Meyer because he was a vampire. He seemed to like it, so Ollis gently poked again.

He was careful not to hurt himself. Even if he did, Meyer wouldn't become a bloodthirsty monster, and he wouldn't attack him, but they weren't there yet. Ollis wasn't ready to let Meyer drink his blood. It felt like something intimate that might happen as they got to know each other better, but it was too soon.

Meyer didn't seem to have a problem with that because he continued kissing Ollis as if his life depended on it. Eventually, they were both breathless, and Ollis felt like he might explode. He was hard in his jeans, but that was okay because he could feel that Meyer was, too.

"That was unexpected," Ollis said with a smile.

Meyer hadn't let go of him, which Ollis hoped meant that the vampire had enjoyed the kiss and wanted many more.

"You kissed me first," Meyer pointed out.

"But I didn't expect you to kiss me back."

"How could I not? You don't see yourself the way others do. You certainly don't see yourself the way *I* do. You might be young, but it doesn't mean you're a fool or that you can't be responsible for the pack while Sloan and Kieran deal with the dragons. I don't care who tells you you're not capable of doing this. Don't believe them, because you are. I'll remind you of it every day if you need me to."

Ollis buried his face against Meyer's neck. This felt intimate, too, but not as much as the thought of drinking blood. Ollis was glad Meyer allowed him to do it and even more grateful for the help Meyer would give him. He still might not be sure he could do this on his own, but he *wasn't* on his own, and he had to remember that.

Chapter Three

"I'm just saying we should take the fight to them instead of waiting for them to attack us," Parker explained.

He was slouched in the chair on the right of Luca's bedroom-slash-cell door. Meyer was in the other chair, wondering why he always ended up here with Parker. He wasn't keeping an eye on Parker and Luca, but it sure looked like he was.

It had been a while since Meyer had spent so much time with his siblings, including Parker. Usually they were scattered around the country, if not the world. They loved each other and were a family, but living as long as they did, they didn't feel the need to spend a lot of time together.

Meyer had missed that. He enjoyed traveling and settling down in different countries and cities, but there was something about talking to his brother face-to-face that was soothing and made him want to stick around. He didn't know what Parker would do once this mess was over, but there was a good chance he and Luca would be together. Luca probably wouldn't want to stay with the pack after the way they treated him, but maybe he'd stay in the area.

And maybe Meyer would, too.

It was too soon to think about it, especially considering their situation. There was no way to know what the dragons would do next or if the pack would survive their attacks. Meyer could only hope.

He'd decided that if it came to it, he'd grab his family, Ollis, and anyone important to both of them and drag them away.

He had enough money to take them to safety, and while he wanted to save the pack, it might not be possible.

Everyone hoped it would be. They acted accordingly, as was right. They needed to fight to show the dragons that people could stand up to them. They'd been unchecked for too long, which Meyer suspected was why they believed they could act with impunity.

They were right to fight, but there was no need for anyone to die for the pack. It was good to have a plan B, although Meyer wasn't sure what Ollis would think of it.

He almost snorted. He *did* know what Ollis would think of it. Ollis wouldn't leave the pack. He wouldn't have before, but now that he was helping Kieran, he'd feel it was his responsibility to stick around and help.

Maybe he was right. Maybe it *was* his responsibility, and Meyer was allowing himself to be distracted by his emotions. He didn't think so and firmly believed the pack should fight, but not at the cost of everyone dying. Surely Kieran wanted his people to survive. He wasn't the kind of person who would sacrifice their lives for the pack, but either way, people would probably die. Meyer didn't imagine that surrendering to the dragons would help much. They wanted blood, and they'd get it.

"You're not listening to me," Parker accused as he pushed Meyer's shoulder.

Meyer tilted sideways, but he didn't fall from his chair. He glared at his brother even though Parker was right—he hadn't been listening. "You think we should attack the dragons instead of waiting for them to attack us," Meyer said. "And while I agree that usually that might be something to consider, how do you suppose we could do it against a whole clan of dragons? It's not like we can attack them one by one. They live together in the same place, and I'm sure security is tight. They won't even let us get close to the house, let alone inside of it."

Parker pouted. "Way to ruin my perfect plan."

"If it had been perfect, we'd be implementing it."

The sound of a door slamming and loud voices made Meyer and Parker jump. They glanced at each other. Meyer knew Parker had to be wondering what was happening like he was.

Parker got to his feet and placed himself in front of the bedroom door while Meyer went down the hallway. He doubted they were under attack—who would be stupid enough to attack a house full of vampires—but something *was* happening.

He almost collided with his brother Rex, who was running up the stairs. Meyer opened his mouth to tell his brother to fuck off, but he didn't get the chance. Rex raised his phone, and Meyer didn't have to look at the screen to know why.

He briefly closed his eyes. He was afraid to ask, and for a moment, he wondered what would happen if he didn't. It was tempting.

"What's wrong?" Parker asked from behind Meyer.

Rex raised his phone. "Have you guys seen the news?"

They hadn't yet, but Rex's expression told Meyer everything he needed to know. "What did they attack this time?"

"A police station."

Meyer frowned. "Why a police station? It doesn't make sense after they attacked the mall." There wouldn't be nearly enough people there for the dragons to be satisfied.

"It does when you realize it's the one at the town center."

Meyer grimaced. A lot of stores and restaurants were located there, and they were always busy. Many people spent time there every day, especially families.

"They want everyone to know they're not afraid of authority," Parker said.

He was already scrolling on his phone, probably to find the latest news. Meyer should be doing the same, but his heart sank at the thought.

Did he need to see what the dragons were doing? He already knew it had resulted in many deaths.

He took his phone out anyway. If there was anything he could do, he wanted to know.

It was clear the dragons knew what they were doing. The alpha was pissed at Kieran, and it would have been easy for him to attack the pack head-on and win. Right now, the pack didn't have enough allies. Even though they could put up a good fight, in the end, they'd lose.

But instead of attacking the pack, the dragons were attacking people who had nothing to do with their fight. They weren't even targeting supernatural people. At the mall, the majority of the people killed were humans, and the same would have happened today. There were many more humans in the world than supernatural creatures.

But maybe the dragons didn't care how many humans they killed. After all, even once the dragons were rid of the pack, there would still be people standing between them and what they wanted. This was a human world. It didn't belong to supernatural creatures. It certainly didn't belong to the dragons, no matter how strong and ruthless they were.

"He's not going to stop," Luca said from inside the bedroom.

He must have been listening to the conversation. Meyer would have been in his place.

"We have to do something," Parker interjected. "Luca, do you have any idea? How do we stop the clan?"

"I wouldn't be locked up in this bedroom if I knew. I can give you as much information as I want, but it won't change the fact that the clan is powerful. They'll do whatever they want for however long they feel like it. There's nothing anyone can do about it."

"Then why did you come here?" Meyer snapped. They

needed people to have faith that they could do *something*, even though it was clear they couldn't. They couldn't allow people to lose hope. If they did, the war would be over.

There was a moment of silence before Luca answered. "I don't know. I knew I was joining the side that would probably lose, but I couldn't live with myself anymore. I didn't try to stop the clan because nothing I could do or say would have, and the next best thing was to leave. Even if I die tomorrow, at least I won't die a clan member. I won't die following the dragon alpha's orders and killing people just because he wants them to die. I had to decide what was more important to me, and I chose not to be ashamed of myself and my actions."

Meyer understood, but that didn't help. They needed to stop the dragons.

How were they supposed to do it?

Ollis eyed Merrick. Did he really need to be there while he and Alpin had coffee? Ollis didn't see a reason for it. He hadn't said a word since they'd arrived. It was as if Ollis didn't matter to him, and while that was probably true, it was kind of rude to be so obvious about it.

"I'd ask why you learned how to make coffee for vampires, but I don't think I need to," Alpin teased.

Ollis turned his attention back to him. "I just wanted to do something nice for you."

Alpin looked like he didn't believe him. "And you like my brother."

What was Ollis supposed to say? He could behave as if he didn't know what Alpin was talking about, but there was a reason Alpin was teasing him. He already knew what was happening between Meyer and Ollis. He was fishing for details, and while Ollis wanted to scream from the rooftops that he and Meyer were together, it was probably better that he didn't.

"All your brothers are nice," he settled on.

Alpin rolled his eyes and took another sip of coffee. "Have it your way. You're my brother-in-law now, though, and that means something to me."

Ollis had been taking a sip of his coffee—without blood for him—and he sputtered into his mug. "Brother-in-law?"

"You and Meyer are together, aren't you?"

"Yes," Ollis admitted. He might as well.

"Which makes you my brother-in-law."

"I think it's too soon to call me that."

Even though it sounded good. Having Alpin call him his brother-in-law made Ollis feel like everything would work out. He and Meyer would continue being together, the war would soon end, and they'd take the next step in their relationship, whatever it was.

"I don't know. It's been a long time since I saw Meyer happy, and considering the circumstances, I feel you're doing a good job."

Ollis had no idea what to say. Should he thank Alpin?

He wasn't doing anything he wouldn't normally do. He and Meyer hadn't spent a lot of time together since Kieran had asked Ollis to become substitute alpha. Ollis hadn't officially started yet, but he would have to soon, so Kieran and Sloan were helping him learn what he needed to know as quickly as he could.

Ollis and Meyer texted every day. They called each other when they had enough time, and even without seeing each other much, Ollis felt close to Meyer. In some ways, being honest while they were on the phone was easier. Ollis didn't know what would come out of it, and he certainly didn't know what would happen with the dragons, but he had one more reason to fight. If he wanted any kind of future with

Meyer, the pack had to win this war.

There was nothing Ollis could do about it. His job wasn't to focus on the dragons. He'd focus on the pack so that Kieran and Sloan could protect them without having to worry. Ollis was sure he could do it, but sometimes, doubt plagued him.

What if he messed up? What if he had to keep calling Kieran or Sloan?

His worst nightmare would be to have someone dismiss him because he wasn't Kieran. Hell, maybe that person would be his brother. It would be just like Malcolm, and Ollis couldn't stop thinking about it.

How would Malcolm treat him when he found out about this? He'd always believed that Ollis was childish and immature, and while it bothered Ollis, it wasn't what annoyed him the most. It was that Malcolm felt superior and wasn't willing to accept that he wasn't. Maybe he would never accept it, and eventually Ollis would stop trying to keep up with their relationship.

Ollis loved his brother, although sometimes, he also hated him. He didn't want anything bad to happen to Malcolm, but maybe it was time to set some boundaries and put space between them. Malcolm would try to ignore them, but Ollis was strong. He could stand up to his older brother.

"Leave him alone," Merrick grumbled. "He doesn't want to answer your questions."

Merrick was drinking a cup of normal coffee, like Ollis. He could have had coffee with blood, but he'd shaken his head when Ollis had tentatively offered him one. Ollis had heard rumors that Merrick wasn't comfortable with his vampire side. Ollis wasn't surprised.

He hadn't thought it was possible to turn a shifter into a vampire before meeting Merrick. Maybe it only worked with dragon shifters, or maybe Merrick was special. Either way, the thought was horrifying. Ollis didn't want to think about the possibility that all shifters could become vampires. It was too scary.

Merrick was both a shifter and a vampire—as if he wasn't intimidating enough already. His arms were so thick with muscles that Ollis wouldn't have been surprised to find out that he tore off the heads of his enemies. The permanent scowl on his face didn't help matters, although Alpin's presence slightly did.

Alpin leaned sideways toward Merrick and smacked a kiss on his cheek. Merrick barely reacted, but Alpin didn't seem to care.

"Don't worry about him," he told Ollis. "He's a big Teddy bear."

Thankfully, Ollis hadn't been drinking this time. *Merrick* was a Teddy bear? Then maybe Ollis was the Pope.

"Stop bothering him," Merrick grumbled.

To Ollis's surprise, the big dragon shifter looked straight at him. "I heard what Sloan and Kieran asked you to do. It took a lot of guts to say yes to their offer."

The rumors had already started spreading, which was a wonder because Ollis couldn't explain how it was possible. Only a handful of people knew what they were planning, and he was sure none would have discussed it.

But people had seen Ollis walk into Kieran's house, so they knew something was up. Some, like Malcolm, believed Ollis was in trouble. Malcolm had already texted Ollis several times to ask what happened and his punishment, but he'd ignored all of his brother's messages. He wasn't about to tell Malcolm what Kieran had wanted by text, if anything because he wanted to see his brother's expression when he realized what it meant.

Ollis almost cackled. He'd never really be the alpha, but he'd have power over his brother through this.

Ollis wouldn't abuse that power. He had every intention of

doing a good job and didn't want Kieran to regret choosing him. He just found it hilarious that his brother was always telling him he was immature and would never amount to anything, and now, he was in charge of the pack.

"I don't know about guts," he told Merrick. "Sometimes, I think I should have said no."

Merrick nodded as if he understood. "You have to ignore the voice that says that you can't do it. Kieran wouldn't have chosen you if he didn't believe in you."

That was the most Merrick had ever spoken to Ollis. Ollis wasn't quite sure how to answer, but maybe he could focus on Merrick being his friend's boyfriend. As long as Alpin and Ollis were friends, Merrick would be part of Ollis's life.

"I've never done anything like this, but I'm ready to learn and do my best. I just hope the pack goes easy on me."

Merrick's eyes narrowed and he growled a little, which seemed to delight Alpin but scared Ollis a little. "Do you think the pack will give you a hard time?"

"I hope not, but a lot of them see me as a kid. Would you take your orders from a child?"

Alpin snorted. "He only takes orders from me."

Merrick patted him on the head as if he were a cat. "You're so short you might as well be a child."

Ollis was in awe. Where had this side of Merrick's personality come from? He let Alpin tease him, and he was even smiling.

Was this what love did to a man? Ollis didn't need or want Meyer to change, but he couldn't wait until the two of them were comfortable enough with each other to have a relationship like the one Merrick and Alpin shared.

He just hoped they would get to that point, but it was hard to believe.

It felt almost wrong to head over to Ollis's house to pick him up for a date after what had happened that day, but that didn't stop Meyer. He needed something good after watching the news for hours.

It had been horrible. The police station the dragons had destroyed was in rubble, and while there were survivors, many people were dead. Kieran had gone there to try and help, but they'd had to return when people realized they were shifters.

It was still odd to think that humans were finally aware of what had been under their nose for so long. They'd been able to ignore it when it had only been a few isolated incidents, but the dragons were done hiding. They were bold when they attacked, showing their faces to the world.

That world was panicking. The dragons had exposed themselves, which was already bad enough. The fact that they were showing the entire world that they were bloodthirsty and cruel was worse. It meant humans were afraid of shifters, even when they weren't dragons.

Humans were afraid of what they didn't understand. Some strived to understand and learn, while others turned stubborn. Those were the worst. Even when presenting them with evidence, they would never believe wolf shifters were different from these dragon shifters. They'd already made their decision—shifters were evil, and that was that.

Nothing could be further from the truth.

In the past, shifters and vampires hadn't gotten along. Some shifters resented the fact that vampires had been human and felt superior because of that. There had been many wars fought between the two groups, and Meyer was glad those wars were over.

Unfortunately, this one wasn't.

As he drove to Ollis's house, he tried to think of a way to use what he knew to defeat the dragons. Unfortunately, he couldn't come up with anything. He couldn't shift into an animal that might give him a slight edge against the dragons. He'd have to face them in this form because it was the only form he had, and even though he was a vampire, the thought was enough to make him want to scream.

He did have some skills when it came to fighting. The problem was that it had been a long time since he'd used those skills, and there were plenty of new weapons around. He still trained with his sword almost every day, but he'd never expected to have to use that ability again.

Sword against dragon. What could go wrong?

So many things that it wasn't funny. Thankfully, Meyer had reached Ollis's house, which meant he could stop obsessing over it. The only thing he wanted to focus on tonight was Ollis and for both of them to have a good time. They couldn't allow the dragons and the impending war to take their lives away. It was what the dragons wanted.

They wanted people to stop fighting so they could take over, and maybe it had worked in the past, but not anymore.

There was another car parked in front of Ollis's house. Meyer had visited a few times, but it was the first time he'd seen someone visiting Ollis. He hesitated, wondering how whoever this was would take his presence. There was no way to know, and he didn't want Ollis to think he was ashamed of him or that he was abandoning him, so he decided to wait.

Maybe he could call or text Ollis to let him know he was out here. Ollis knew Meyer was coming, which meant he might be trying to get rid of his visitor. If that was the case, Meyer could help.

A lot of shifters in the pack were still wary of him and his siblings. They weren't used to vampires, and just like Meyer, they'd always been told that vampires and shifters were enemies. Maybe they were starting to see that wasn't the case, or maybe not. Either way, Meyer already knew they weren't enemies, which hopefully meant they were one step closer to accepting each other.

Meyer quickly texted Ollis that he'd arrived, then got out of the car. He expected the door to open, maybe so that the visitor could leave, but it remained stubbornly closed. Ollis also didn't answer Meyer's text, which meant Meyer had to take the next step.

A knock on the door.

He did just that, wondering what Ollis would look like when he opened it. This was their first official date, and although they weren't doing anything remarkable, Meyer wanted to look good for Ollis. That was why he wore a nice pair of dress pants and a classic sweater. It felt like it might be too much, but Ollis wouldn't care.

When the door finally opened, Ollis wasn't the one standing behind it. Meyer and the man stared at each other for a moment, and Meyer tried to remember if he'd seen him before. He looked somewhat familiar, but Meyer didn't realize why until Ollis appeared behind him.

He wore a dark pair of nice jeans and a sweater, but that wasn't what got Meyer's attention. He also wore a thunderous expression that could only have to do with the man separating him from Meyer.

"You're one of the vampires," the man said.

Meyer nodded curtly. "I'm Meyer."

"What are you doing here?"

"It's none of your business," Ollis snapped as he tried to push past the guy. "Now, will you leave? I have nothing to say to you."

"You could try telling me the truth," the unknown man said.

Meyer had no idea who the guy was, but he was starting to get irritated with him. Hadn't he heard Ollis? He needed to get the fuck out.

"I can't tell you anything. Kieran will make an

announcement, and until then, that's all you need to know."

"You're in trouble, aren't you? That's why he called you to his office."

Meyer cleared his throat. "I believe Ollis told you it was none of your business and that you needed to leave."

The man looked surprised that Meyer was talking to him. "I can talk to my brother if I want to."

Meyer narrowed his eyes. Ollis had told him about Malcolm a few times, and nothing he'd said had endeared the man to Meyer. He sounded boring and annoying, and that was without considering the way he treated Ollis.

"Only if your brother wants to talk to you, and it's clear he doesn't," Meyer said.

"Besides, I have something to do," Ollis said as he pushed Malcolm forward. "Meyer and I are going on a date."

Instead of getting Malcolm to finally move, the words made him freeze in his tracks. "You're dating a vampire?" he asked, sounding scandalized.

Meyer was pleased by the realization that he'd made Malcolm uncomfortable. He'd barely talked to the man, but he already found him insufferable. He wanted to make him squirm and to make him regret the way he'd treated Ollis all these years.

Ollis crossed his arms over his chest. "Yes, I'm dating a vampire. What's it to you?"

"You can't do that."

"Why not?"

"Because he's a vampire."

Malcolm made it sound as if that was explanation enough. Meyer knew that for many people, it would be. Even if he ignored the fact that he was a vampire and Ollis was a shifter, a lot of people were wary of vampires. They expected them to attack at any moment and drink them dry.

That wasn't physically possible. An average human body

would have about 160 ounces of blood, and a normal stomach could only hold about 34 ounces, maybe 50 if it stretched completely. Even if a vampire drank so much that he overfed, it would be hard to kill someone just by feeding on them. Of course, that didn't mean vampires didn't kill humans. They did so all the time, just like humans and shifters killed humans. There were evil and cruel people in all species.

"I'm aware," Ollis said. "Can you leave? We have to go."

"You can't be with a vampire," Malcolm insisted. "He's going to hurt you."

"How would he hurt me? He wouldn't be here if Kieran didn't trust him."

"Kieran's father would never have allowed vampires in our territory."

"Kieran's father was an abusive asshole. If you have nothing nice to say, Malcolm, you can leave. In fact, I insist you do so because I have somewhere to be, and it's much nicer than here because you won't be there."

Ollis was proud of himself for standing up to Malcolm, but he really wished his brother had chosen any other moment to be an asshole.

He already knew Malcolm wouldn't like the fact that he was dating a vampire. He didn't care, especially since he'd never thought of Malcolm when he'd chosen who to date. It was none of Malcolm's business, even though Malcolm always tried to make it his.

Ollis had almost yelled at Malcolm when his brother had arrived without calling first. He'd told Ollis that he was missing him and wanted to see him, but Ollis had known all along that Malcolm wanted to find out why Ollis had been seen talking to Kieran and Sloan.

It wasn't a surprise that people wondered. They might not

know about Kieran and Sloan's decision, but they had eyes and saw that Ollis was spending a lot more time with the alpha and beta since their meeting. It should also be clear that it wasn't a punishment, but it looked like they only saw what they wanted to see. They thought of Ollis as a troublemaker, so of course he had to be in trouble.

Right now, he was mostly in trouble with his brother. Malcolm was staring at him as if he'd sprouted another head.

"But why him?" Malcolm insisted. "I'm sure you have plenty of options. You don't have to stoop so low."

Ollis growled and took a step forward. Malcolm's eyes widened, maybe because he hadn't expected Ollis to react. He usually didn't. He'd learned long ago that reacting to his brother's teasing would only bring pain. Malcolm didn't hurt him physically, but it didn't mean he couldn't hurt Ollis with his words.

That was what he was trying to do right now. Maybe he wasn't trying to *hurt* Ollis, but that was what his words were doing.

"I'm dating Meyer because I like him and want to date *him*, not someone else," Ollis said as he tried to stay calm. "That's all you need to know. Can you leave now?"

"But why a vampire?"

"I don't care what Meyer is. I just care that he's Meyer, and I like him." Ollis was losing his patience, but Malcolm wasn't done pushing. He wouldn't be until he got what he wanted, but Ollis wasn't planning on giving it to him.

"Well, I suppose you have even fewer options than I thought," Malcolm said. "Who would want to be with you when you have nothing to offer? Maybe this guy thinks you'll let him drink from you if he takes you out, but be careful."

Ollis was horrified. He couldn't believe Malcolm had just said that he wasn't good enough to date Meyer. Even though he could be right, it wasn't his place to say something like that, and he definitely shouldn't have said it in front of Meyer.

Ollis looked at his boyfriend. He half expected Meyer to agree with Malcolm and leave, and for a moment, he thought that was what would happen. Meyer looked pissed, and it could be because Malcolm was right.

Ollis should have known better. Meyer was a sweetheart who didn't care about other people's thoughts. He certainly didn't care about Malcolm's opinion. In fact, he looked like he wanted to pummel Malcolm into the ground. It was tempting to let him do it, but that wouldn't be the best way to start Ollis's new job. Besides, he didn't want Malcolm to be hurt. He just wanted his brother to stay out of his life, and he didn't think it was too much to ask.

Thankfully, Meyer seemed to feel the same way. He sucked in a breath and visibly centered himself, then turned to Ollis. "Are you ready to go?"

"Let me grab my phone and wallet."

Meyer nodded. Even though Ollis wanted to ask him to come in, he didn't. He ignored Malcolm trailing after him as he went back to the kitchen to grab his phone, but he should have known Malcolm wouldn't let it go. He never did, no matter how many times his daughters watched that cartoon. He could learn a lot from Elsa.

"I know there aren't a lot of people out there for you, but you can still do better," Malcolm insisted.

Ollis snorted. "Can I? Because from how you talk about me, it sounds like no one in the world is worse than me. Why would anyone want to date me if that's the case?"

Malcolm winced. Maybe he hadn't realized how hurtful his words could be. It would be the first time he cared, but Ollis could hope it wouldn't be the last.

"You're not the worst," Malcolm said as Ollis turned off the light. "You don't have to lower yourself to date a vampire. We can ask around town, since I know there's no one for you in the pack."

Ollis could still see Meyer on the porch, but it looked like his boyfriend wouldn't step in. This was a problem Ollis needed to solve by himself, and while he felt he couldn't, he was done doing this with Malcolm. He was done with Malcolm, period. If his brother had nothing nice to say, he could stop talking.

"I don't want to find anyone else. I don't care that Meyer is a vampire, and I don't think that what he is makes a difference. I like him. I like how sweet and supportive he is."

"You don't need him! You have your family to support you."

"Except you haven't supported me one day in your life. You're always going on about how I should find someone, settle down, have kids, and finally be an adult, but when I do it, you tell me it's still not good enough. I tried so hard, but I've come to the conclusion that nothing I do will ever be enough for you, and you know what? That's fine with me. I'm done trying to impress you. I'm done trying to make you love me. If you can't accept me the way I am, you never will, and even though that hurts, it's all right. I can deal with not having you in my life."

Malcolm's eyes were wide and he looked like he was about to argue, which was the last thing Ollis wanted. He grabbed his brother's arm and pulled him toward the front door where Meyer was waiting. Malcolm shut his mouth and skirted around Meyer as if he feared Meyer would attack him. Thankfully, even if Meyer was offended, he didn't say anything about it. He rolled his eyes at Malcolm before turning his attention to Ollis.

"You look handsome tonight."

Ollis told himself he wasn't going to blush, but it wasn't easy. "So do you."

Malcolm made a strangled sound. Meyer and Ollis

continued ignoring him. He didn't deserve one more second of their attention, and Ollis wasn't going to think of him again tonight.

He might regret some of the things he'd said tomorrow, but it had been overdue. If Malcolm hadn't wanted to hear them, he should have treated Ollis better.

Ollis locked the door after grabbing his jacket. "Lead the way."

"Ollis," Malcolm began, but one glare from Ollis was enough for him to snap his mouth shut.

Ollis didn't care if his brother stayed on his porch for the rest of the night. As long as he didn't have to be there with him, it didn't matter. He doubted Malcolm would do it, anyway. He had a family to go back to.

Ollis and Meyer climbed into the car, and as soon as he was out of sight of his brother, Ollis closed his eyes and sighed deeply.

"How long has he been bothering you?" Meyer asked.

"He got here about fifteen minutes before you did. I tried telling him he needed to leave, but he ignored me. Even though he could see I was dressed for a date, he acted as if it just wasn't possible."

"Has he always been like that?"

"You mean, has he always told me I wasn't good enough?"

Meyer's jaw tightened. "Yes."

"I know that telling you not to worry about him would be useless, but seriously. You don't have to be angry at him. I don't care what he thinks, and I'm done trying to justify my life and choices. Nothing he can do or say will hurt me again." Or at least, Ollis hoped so. Malcolm was his brother, though, and he had the capacity to hurt him more than almost anyone else in the world.

Meyer turned in his seat and gently squeezed the back of Ollis's neck. "I don't want to be out of place or condescending, but you must know you *are* enough. You're enough for me. You'd be enough for anyone. You're smart, sweet, caring, and gentle. You don't deserve what your brother said, but you do deserve someone who will love you."

Ollis sucked in a breath. "Could that someone be you?"

Meyer didn't hesitate. "It already is."

Chapter Four

Meyer and his family huddled together, surrounded as they were by wolf shifters. Meyer wasn't sure it was a good idea for them to be present, but Kieran hadn't been wrong when he'd pointed out they were pack members. He'd welcomed them into the pack, and they were supposed to be there if there was a pack meeting.

The only one missing was Parker. He was back at the house guarding Luca, and Meyer could imagine what kind of trouble the two of them were getting up to. Parker was spending more and more time with Luca. They were separated by a door, but Meyer doubted that changed anything. His brother had an unfortunate crush on the dragon, and eventually, their situation would reach a breaking point. Meyer didn't know what would happen when it did.

He believed Luca wanted to help the pack. He'd made the hard choice of leaving his clan. It would have been easier for him to fly away and never look back. Instead, he'd decided to help the pack, but as of now, the pack hadn't accepted that help. Meyer wasn't sure why they were keeping him here. If they didn't want anything to do with him, they might as well let him go. That way, he'd have a chance to save himself.

But so far, Kieran hadn't given any orders regarding Luca, which meant Meyer and his family would keep guarding him. Parker volunteered most of the time, and Meyer wondered if he should talk to their father about it.

Tyrian was there, huddled close to his boyfriend, Madison. People kept glancing at them, and Madison looked like he wanted to run. That was understandable since first, he'd been forced to leave the pack, and then he'd had to choose between his sister and betraying Kieran. Everyone knew what he'd done—or rather, hadn't done—and they were all curious.

Madison wasn't the only person people were staring at. Every member of Meyer's family probably felt like they were in the spotlight. Some dealt with it better than others. Baxter was hovering by the door, almost as if he was about to run. He might have if he wasn't dating Sloan, the beta. Rex and Umberto seemed unconcerned by what everyone else was doing. Their conversation was so focused that Meyer wondered if they'd even hear Kieran when he started talking.

"Hey," Ollis said, appearing next to Meyer.

Meyer couldn't stop himself from smiling. He wanted to pull Ollis into his arms and kiss him, but that probably wasn't the best idea. Most of the pack had to know they were together by now, but tonight's announcement was all about Ollis, so Meyer didn't want to ruin everything for him. He'd let Ollis decide what he was ready for.

Ollis hesitated, then took Meyer's hand and squeezed. "I'm so nervous I feel I could throw up."

Meyer squeezed back. It wasn't a kiss, but it was more than he'd expected. "Breathe."

"I've been trying to, but I'm panicking."

"You'll do fine. Just focus on the work you've been doing with Kieran and Sloan and on the trust they have in you. What the others think doesn't matter. They chose *you*, and that's the only thing that does."

Ollis nodded, but he still looked a little green. Unfortunately for him, Meyer noticed Kieran and Sloan entering the room.

When he'd been told there would be a pack meeting, he'd wondered where they'd do it. Not everyone had come, since some people were stuck at work or at home for various reasons, but most of the pack members were present, and the place was crowded.

He didn't know pack territory well yet. He spent a lot of time either guarding Luca or patrolling the territory, but like the other guards, he stayed at the perimeter. The territory was larger than he'd expected, and it included this community building.

It looked like most of the time, children and families used it. Tables and chairs had been stacked to the side, along with a bunch of toys. The children were playing with some of them, with a few people keeping an eye on them. Madison's sister was one of those children, which explained why he was here, exposing himself to everyone's gaze. Or maybe he'd decided to come because he was a pack member like everyone else. He'd left because he'd been forced to, not because he'd wanted to.

A small stage seemed to be regularly used for something artistic. There were props and landscapes pushed toward the back, but they wouldn't need those tonight.

Kieran and Sloan climbed onto the stage. Meyer noticed both Baxter and Robin move closer, and it was good to see that people didn't step away from Robin like Meyer might have expected. No one hugged him or came too close, but most of the people he walked past nodded at him and said hello.

It looked like the pack was slowly starting to accept their new vampire members. It gave Meyer hope that he and Ollis could have a peaceful life here.

As soon as they got rid of the dragons, anyway.

"Good evening, everyone," Kieran said, his voice booming.

The conversations quieted, and people turned their attention to their alpha. Meyer had been seeing Kieran often since Ollis was spending a lot of time with him, and he'd looked tired and at the end of his rope, but not anymore. Tonight, he looked like an alpha, and Meyer could feel it in the way the people in the room reacted.

"Since I'm sure everyone has better things to do than listen to me, I'm going to get straight to the point," Kieran announced. "You all know about the dragons and the danger they represent to our pack. You know what they did at the mall and, more recently, at the police station. Unfortunately, they've decided we're their enemy, and while they haven't focused on the pack yet, I believe it's only a matter of time before they do. Sloan and I've been working hard to find the best way to protect all of you and our territory, and we came to the conclusion that we need more allies. We have some, but it's not enough."

Kieran paused and looked around. The room was completely silent. Ollis was squeezing Meyer's hand to the point of pain, but Meyer didn't make him stop. His boyfriend was nervous, and Meyer would do whatever he could to make him feel better. He needed to make a good impression once Kieran explained everything. Ollis had a bit of a reputation and was nervous that people wouldn't give him a chance.

Meyer looked around, trying to locate Ollis's brother. Thankfully, he was on the other side of the room, but instead of looking at Kieran, his attention was on Ollis. A woman stood next to him, holding a little girl.

Meyer caught his eye and arched a brow. Malcolm pressed his lips together and looked away, but Meyer suspected it wouldn't be long until he was staring again.

Kieran was still talking, so Meyer turned his focus back on him.

"We have found several people who would be good allies, but they want to talk to us. That means leaving pack territory, which is something we've been trying to avoid but can't anymore. Sloan and I both need to sit in these meetings because the future of the pack depends on them and because some of these people want to talk to both of us. Even when we're in pack territory, all of this is taking a lot of time and focus, and I feel I don't have enough time to dedicate to the pack's everyday problems."

This was it. Ollis was about to be called on stage. He was slightly shaking, and unfortunately, Meyer could do nothing about it.

"Which is why Sloan and I have chosen someone to help temporarily. He won't be the alpha, but he *will* be the person you can go to if you have any kind of trouble or problem. He'll have full authority to make decisions when it comes to the pack until this mess is over, and of course, he'll keep Sloan and me updated."

Kieran looked around, no doubt to find Ollis. Ollis took a deep breath, squared his shoulders, and let go of Meyer's hand. He didn't go right away, so Meyer leaned closer to him.

"You can do this," he whispered.

Ollis nodded once. "I can."

"Ollis?" Kieran called out. "Can you come up on the stage?"

Ollis looked like he'd rather not, but he stepped forward.

Ollis felt like he might faint. Either that, or he'd run.

It took everything he had to force his shaking legs to take him up on the stage. He ignored the crowd of people behind him because if he didn't, he'd freak out and do something stupid. He needed the pack to trust him and to see him as someone they could come to when they had a problem. He had to make sure they didn't think he was an idiot.

But he was dying to find his brother in the crowd and see how he'd taken the news. He was probably gaping. If Ollis knew him, he couldn't believe what Kieran had just said, but there was no denying the alpha's choice. He'd chosen Ollis, and Ollis would do him proud.

He got onto the stage and went to stand next to Sloan and Kieran. Kieran turned back to the crowd, but Sloan leaned closer to Ollis. "Look at the back of the room," he whispered. "It's the best way not to freak out."

Ollis nodded slightly and did as Sloan suggested. It was the first time he'd stood under the attention of so many people. His heart raced, and his palms were sweaty.

"Unless it concerns the dragons, I want you to go to Ollis for anything you might need," Kieran said. "He has Sloan's and my trust, and while we'll keep in touch with him, we trust him to make decisions for the pack. If neither of us is here, Ollis will be your alpha. If we are present, he'll still be the person you need to go to. I'm sure many of you have questions, and I'll be right here to answer as many as possible, but Sloan and I won't change our mind. Things are hard enough already. Please, don't make them harder by fighting us over this."

Kieran was done. He turned to Ollis and gestured at the crowd, possibly asking if Ollis wanted to say something. Ollis couldn't think of a worse idea, so he quickly shook his head, which caused Kieran to grin.

Sloan slapped Ollis on the back. "You'll do a good job. We went over everything, and you're ready. Besides, remember that this is only temporary."

That was a relief, because Ollis wasn't sure what he would have done if he'd had to become the actual alpha. Probably run away screaming and hide in the woods for the rest of his life.

The three of them climbed off the stage, and Ollis steeled himself. People would want to talk to him. If anything, they'd be curious and have questions, which he hoped he was ready for. He'd prepared a bunch of answers, but it depended on what people would do.

They were his pack, and he needed to have faith in them. He prayed they wouldn't react the way Malcolm surely had. He was about to find out.

The first person stepped in front of him, and he plastered a smile on his face. Mrs. Jensen was one of the elders of the pack. It didn't hold any official meaning, but the pack respected them.

"Well, I can't say I expected this," she said.

"You're not the only one," Ollis blurted out. He swallowed and told himself to be more relaxed. "I know that this role is supposed to go to the alpha mate, but Robin didn't feel comfortable doing so."

She nodded. "That's understandable. In this role, you want people to have full faith in you and the decisions you make." She tsked. "I think it's ridiculous that people don't trust Robin, but they will eventually. In the meantime, you're a fine choice."

Ollis could have kissed her. "You think so?"

"I always thought you were a nice boy, and you turned into a nice man. I have faith in you, Ollis, and I'm not the only one. Good luck." She snickered. "You'll need it."

She was right, and Ollis should probably be more worried, but he couldn't find it in himself to feel that way. She was the first of the pack to talk to him after the announcement, and she trusted him.

The people who came after her didn't all feel the same, but most seemed accepting of Kieran's decision. Some appeared confused, probably because Ollis hadn't been close to Kieran before, but they trusted their alpha, which meant they trusted Ollis.

Mostly, anyway.

Having so many people who wanted to talk to him was overwhelming, but Ollis tried to stay calm. This was only the first day, and he had to get used to it. He was a little stunned that some people already wanted him to solve their problems, but he could do it. He was sure of it.

Eventually, his parents appeared in front of him. He swallowed, not knowing how they'd react. He should have told them, but he hadn't wanted them to know until he and Kieran were ready to announce it. Ollis wasn't sure he would ever have actually been ready, but they hadn't been able to wait any longer.

"You didn't tell us," Ollis's father said with a grunt.

Ollis's mother pushed him aside to throw herself into Ollis's arms. "We're so proud of you," she said. "None of us expected it, but we're proud."

Ollis hugged her hard. Even though his parents hadn't always treated him the way he felt they should have, he loved them, and they'd accepted him when it most mattered. Seeing how proud they were mattered and made his eyes burn with tears he didn't want to shed.

"Are we sure Kieran isn't drunk or something?" Malcolm asked from behind their parents. "Because this choice doesn't make sense. Why would he pick Ollis, of all people? Even if he didn't want his boyfriend to be in charge, I can think of a dozen people who would have been better."

Ollis gritted his teeth. Couldn't his brother give him at least this? Did he really have to be like this, even in this situation?

Their mother turned to Malcolm. "Stop being so mean to your brother. Kieran didn't choose *you*, did he?"

Malcolm's cheeks flushed. "I wouldn't have wanted him to. I'm surprised Ollis agreed. We all know he's going to mess this up."

"There's a good reason your alpha chose him instead of you or anyone else here," Meyer snapped.

Ollis hadn't seen him walk up, and he knew he should stop him from tearing into his brother, but he was tired.

No matter how many times he talked to Malcolm, Malcolm

didn't seem to understand. Even now, he seemed to believe that Ollis wasn't good enough. It hurt, and while Ollis wouldn't have said anything about it because there was no reason to, it felt good to have Meyer defend him. Ollis should do it himself, and he'd have to talk to his brother eventually, but not today.

"I wasn't talking to you," Malcolm said. "You're not part of our family."

"Meyer is my boyfriend. He has every right to be involved in this conversation," Ollis said. "Besides, you pulled him into it. Did you really think he was going to stand by and listen to you belittle me?"

Malcolm's cheeks were flushed, and he looked around as if to check no one was listening in.

Meyer's voice rose, and while he wasn't yelling, Ollis noticed several people turn their heads in their direction. "Kieran and Sloan chose the person they believed would be best suited for the role, and that person is your brother. I believe that means he's better than you, contrary to what you've been telling him."

"Can you stop yelling?" Malcolm whispered.

"I'm not yelling. I'm telling you the truth, and it's time you accepted it. You always accuse Ollis of being childish, but I only see one person acting like a child here, and it's not him."

Malcolm's cheeks were so red that Ollis wondered if his head was about to explode. His heart hurt for his brother and the shame he clearly felt, but he also felt vindicated. Malcolm had been like this since they were kids. He'd never hesitated to berate Ollis in front of people or make him feel stupid, and maybe it was time he had a little taste of what he did almost daily.

Malcolm grabbed his wife's hand and pulled her away. "We're leaving," he said.

She didn't argue, but when she and Ollis looked at each

other, she winked and mouthed that she'd call him later. The two of them weren't friends, but they'd grown close over the years, and Ollis was relieved to see he had her support.

He looked around the room. He had a lot more support than he could ever have expected.

Meyer hadn't meant to send Malcolm running, but he was glad the idiot had left. He shouldn't have made a scene and hoped Ollis would forgive him.

He turned to his boyfriend. "I'm sorry about that. I shouldn't have stepped in, but I hate how he talks to you."

Ollis squeezed Meyer's arm. "I'm not mad. No matter how often I stand up for myself, he never hears anything I say. Maybe this time, he'll finally realize what he's been doing all these years."

Ollis's mother cleared her throat. "Your father and I should have stepped in, and I'm sorry we didn't."

This wasn't the best way for Meyer to be introduced to Ollis's parents, but it was done now. He could only weather the storm, and if it meant standing by Ollis's side, he had no problem doing it.

"It's fine," Ollis said.

His father shook his head. "It's not. We always felt it was teasing between brothers, but clearly, it was much more serious. I should have said something sooner. I'm sorry we didn't, Ollis, and I want you to know that we're proud of you. We have no doubt you'll succeed in whatever challenge Kieran throws your way."

Ollis groaned. "Can we not talk about challenges? I'm going to start freaking out if I think about what all of this means."

Ollis's mother hugged him again. "You don't have a reason to freak out. You'll be great at this, Ollis. Everyone is cheering for you, and if even one pack member shows you any disrespect, I'll have a little chat with them."

Meyer smiled. That was a threat many people wouldn't want to deal with. He didn't know Ollis's mother, but she was on her son's side and seemed ready to defend him fiercely.

"Now, what were you saying about your boyfriend?" she asked, turning her attention to Meyer.

He swallowed and told himself he wasn't going to run. No matter how scary Ollis's mother was, it was nothing next to some of the people Meyer had dealt with in his life. He'd faced hydras and dragons. Ollis's mother was just a tiny woman who could turn into a wolf.

Ollis grinned. "This is Meyer, my boyfriend. We haven't been together long, but he's great."

Ollis's mother stared at Meyer. "He sure seems to be. He defended you from your brother, so I'm glad to see you had support when your father and I were too blind to see what we needed to do."

"I believe I could see things more clearly because I'm not part of your family," Meyer said as he lightly bowed and kissed her hand.

He noticed Ollis rolling his eyes, but his mother seemed pleased, so Meyer knew he'd done the right thing. He needed their first meeting to leave a good impression.

He shook Ollis's father's hand, then stepped back. He wasn't sure what to do next. Luckily, he didn't have to wonder for long. People kept coming to Ollis to talk to him, and while Meyer stood close, he never intervened. He didn't have to. Ollis was doing his job, and it was a pleasure to see. He looked sure of himself in a way Meyer hadn't seen him be yet, and he hoped Ollis would continue feeling this way.

Thankfully, it was getting late for the wolves, so the meeting didn't last long. To Meyer, this was only the beginning of the evening, but everyone else had normal schedules, so they wanted to have dinner and go to bed. That meant that after about half an hour, he and Ollis were able to leave.

Meyer waited until they were alone, walking toward the house he shared with his family. He needed to apologize but didn't want to do so in front of people he barely knew.

"I shouldn't have stepped in like I did with your brother," he said. "I'm not sorry I defended you, but I can see that maybe I shouldn't have. You're more than capable of defending yourself."

They were holding hands, and Ollis squeezed Meyer's. "You know, until recently, I wouldn't have thought I was capable of defending myself, especially not from Malcolm. It's always harder when it's your family, isn't it?"

"That's because they matter to you. You don't care about what most people think because they don't matter, at least not the way your brother does. I hope he'll come around, but I'm sorry if I made things worse between the two of you."

Ollis shrugged. "I'm not sure you could have made them worse even if you'd tried. Malcolm has been an asshole most of our lives, but I thought he'd eventually outgrow it. He seems to be stuck in a teenager mentality, though. He teases and behaves as if he's trying to be the most popular kid in school, but this isn't school. This is our family, and I'm afraid if he doesn't understand that, I'm going to lose him."

Meyer didn't know how to help Ollis with Malcolm. The possibility of losing his brother had to hurt, even though Ollis's expression was calm. Meyer had experience with siblings, but it wasn't the same as Ollis and Malcolm. He and his siblings had become close as adults. They weren't related by blood but by the fact that Tyrian had turned all of them, and not growing up together meant they'd never had to deal with the kind of behavior Ollis had.

"I don't want to talk about Malcolm anymore," Ollis said as he glanced at Meyer. "He'll make the decision he needs to make, and there's nothing I can do about that."

Meyer pressed his lips together. "What do you want to talk about, then? How the evening went? I think it's clear that most people trust you."

"It was a surprise. I thought they all still saw me as a troublemaker, but they don't seem to."

"That's because they can see you grew up. Even your parents believe you'll do a good job." Meyer hadn't expected it since they'd never stepped in when Malcolm had teased Ollis. He'd been afraid they felt the way Malcolm did, but it was clear now that they never had.

Ollis grinned. "I can't believe this. Some people have already told me they need to see me soon. I had to tell them to call me tomorrow so I could schedule an appointment. I'm not sure I'm going to like any of this, but I'll do it anyway."

"That's the sign of a good alpha. I don't think Kieran ever wanted the same kind of power his father had, but he still took charge of the pack because that was the best thing for them. He's a good alpha, and I know you'll be of great support to him."

"I just hope I won't make a mess."

It would take time for Ollis to believe he could do this, but he was starting to, and it was a delight to see. "You won't. You have plenty of people ready to help you with anything you might need, Ollis. You're not doing this alone."

"I know. Anyway, I don't want to talk about this anymore."

Meyer was amused. "What do you want to talk about?"

"Well, it looks like you've decided I'll spend the night with you, since we're headed to your place."

Meyer couldn't have stopped smiling even if he tried. "I don't know. You're going to have to go to sleep soon."

"Not that soon. I asked Kieran how he and Robin make it work, and he was happy to tell me. It's not hard. He goes to bed later than most people would and sleeps late in the morning. Everyone's been warned about his new schedule, and I'll tell people the same goes for me. Besides, I don't have appointments tomorrow. People will start calling me, but I can answer their calls from your bed."

"So you planned this."

Meyer was delighted. Considering the circumstances, he'd been ready to take things slow. He didn't want to rush Ollis into anything, but it looked like he shouldn't have been afraid. Ollis knew what he wanted and was ready to take it. Luckily for Meyer, Ollis wanted *him*.

Ollis had been planning and thinking about how they could make their relationship work. Unless Meyer was wrong, Ollis was ready to implement the changes they needed on a permanent basis. That meant he was planning on spending a lot of time with Meyer.

Which was precisely what Meyer wanted.

Ollis *had* planned it and was relieved that Meyer seemed all right with it. They hadn't spent nearly enough time together since they'd become a couple, and things wouldn't get any easier considering the circumstances. They needed to take time together when they could, and today, they could.

Ollis didn't know what to expect, but he trusted Meyer. Whatever happened between them tonight, he was fine with it. He wanted Meyer, and he knew Meyer wanted him.

Ollis needed a few hours away. His mind spun from everything that had happened. Not only had he met Meyer and they'd gotten together, but Kieran had chosen him as a substitute alpha. He was supposed to take care of the pack for him and protect it when he was away. He'd have to solve problems and anticipate trouble, and it was hard to believe that of all the people in the pack, he was the one in charge. For whatever reason, Kieran trusted *him*, and Ollis would show him he deserved that trust.

But not tonight. Tonight, Ollis would focus on Meyer and their relationship. He probably wouldn't have a lot of time to do so later, and he didn't want Meyer to regret being with him or supporting him through all of it. He needed to make sure Meyer knew how much he appreciated him and, even more importantly, how much he wanted him.

He couldn't remember a time when he'd wanted someone more. He didn't often have relationships, and when he did, they were nothing like what he and Meyer had. Ollis still wasn't sure what to make of it, but he didn't need to be. Meyer would give him whatever he needed when he needed it. He was that kind of person, and Ollis was lucky to have met him and even luckier that Meyer had chosen him. It might not make sense, but nothing in Ollis's life did right now, so who cared?

Certainly not Ollis.

"How long do you think your family is going to be out?" he asked.

"Probably for the rest of the night. They enjoy the kind of meeting Kieran organized, and a few of them told me they wanted to go into town when it was over. The only one who will probably be at the house is Parker, but thankfully, my bedroom is away from Luca's."

Ollis's stomach churned. "Maybe we should go to my house."

"We can do whatever you want," Meyer promised.

Ollis doubted anyone would say anything about what he and Meyer were about to do, even if they heard something. Meyer's family wasn't like that. That didn't mean Ollis wouldn't want the earth to swallow him if anyone did hear anything.

But as much as he loved his home, it was isolated, and

sometimes, he didn't feel entirely safe there. He'd chosen it when he'd moved out of the house where he lived with his family because he'd wanted space, and he still did, but with everything happening, sometimes, the house felt a bit too dangerous. He hated not feeling safe in his home, and he hoped it would change again once the war was over, but for now, he would rather stay closer to the center of the pack.

He sighed. "Let's go to your place. If anyone hears anything, I hope they won't tease us."

"Some of my siblings might. My father will make sure they don't go overboard, though."

"Can't they do that themselves? They're adults."

"They are, but sometimes, it's easy to forget how to behave with people. We tend to spend a lot of time on our own, especially some of my siblings. Umberto, for example, has a home in Italy, and when he goes there, he vanishes for decades. He starts reading his books, and he only goes out to feed. Our father always gets worried when he doesn't hear from him for a few years and goes to find him, but living as long as we do, we sometimes need to be away from people."

Ollis wasn't sure he understood. The pack was his home and his family, and he didn't want to be away from them. They were a lot to deal with sometimes, but not so much that he wanted to escape to another country.

But tonight, the house would be mostly empty, and since it was large enough to have private bedrooms for all the siblings and Tyrian, no one would bother them. Ollis clung to that knowledge as they reached the house and Meyer opened the door for him. He smiled and stepped in, hesitating once he stood in the entrance. He knew where Meyer's bedroom was but didn't want to appear presumptuous.

Meyer grabbed his hand after closing the door and pulled him toward the stairs. Ollis laughed, delighted to finally have a more lighthearted moment with his boyfriend.

Everything had been so urgent since they'd gotten together. They couldn't change that, but tonight was just for them. Ollis would try not to think about what would happen tomorrow and about the many responsibilities on his shoulders. Tonight, he was just Ollis, and everything in his life was perfect.

"Do you need anything from the kitchen?" Meyer asked as they climbed the stairs. "There's food for Madison, but I'm sure he wouldn't mind if you ate something."

Ollis shook his head. "Maybe later."

Meyer grinned, exposing his fangs. Seeing them sent a shiver down Ollis's back. Would Meyer use them tonight? He'd never do so without asking Ollis first, but did Ollis *want* him to use them?

He was dating a vampire. There was no ignoring that, and Ollis wasn't planning to. He didn't like Meyer despite of what he was. He liked Meyer *for* who he was, and that was a vampire. Blood and biting would always be part of their lives.

Was Ollis ready for it? He wasn't sure, but he wanted to think he was. He wanted to give all of himself to Meyer, and he knew that Meyer would cherish it, including his blood. Why wouldn't Ollis let Meyer drink from him? There was nothing scary about it because it was Meyer.

Once they were in Meyer's room and Meyer had locked the door, Ollis hesitated. He'd had a plan up until now, but he didn't know what would happen next.

Meyer's hands landed on Ollis's shoulders. "Relax. I don't expect anything from you."

Ollis turned and scowled. "Maybe I expect things from myself."

"I'm sure you do, but you can do whatever you feel like doing in this bedroom with me. If you want to spend the rest of the night watching movies in bed, we can do that."

Ollis loved that Meyer was so careful with him but also that he made it sound like this choice was natural. It was almost as if he truly hadn't expected anything from the evening, which Ollis found hard to believe. People always expected things from their relationships, didn't they?

But Meyer was a vampire. He had all the time in the world, which probably was why he didn't feel the need to rush anything. Whatever the reason, it was clear that watching movies would be an entirely acceptable evening to him.

But not for Ollis. He wanted this, dammit. He wanted to be with Meyer and to stop worrying about everything for a few hours. He was sure Meyer could help him with that, and he couldn't wait.

He wrapped his arms around Meyer's neck. "No movies," he murmured.

Meyer grinned again. "No movies," he agreed before leaning down to kiss Ollis.

Ollis loved that Meyer was never super careful about his fangs when they kissed. Ollis knew they were there, and he'd gotten used to them. He knew that they were sensitive and that he had to be careful not to cut his tongue. Nothing bad would happen if he did except for some pain, but he needed his tongue tonight, so it had to be in working order.

"What do you want, then?" Meyer asked as he gently pushed Ollis toward the bed.

Ollis dropped onto the mattress. "You." He grabbed his sweater and pulled it over his head. He hadn't bothered with a jacket since the weather was warming, even though it was still cool. He was glad he hadn't now. It was one less piece of clothing to take off.

When he freed his head from the sweater, it was to find Meyer watching him with a hungry expression. He was just standing there, still wearing his clothes and watching Ollis. Something squirmed in Ollis's stomach, making him want to cover up and do more at the same time.

First times were always odd. Ollis didn't know what Meyer wanted or what he liked, and the same went for Meyer. They had to find a way to work together, and they would. It was reassuring to know that this was Meyer, though. If Ollis made a fool of himself, Meyer wouldn't care. He wouldn't laugh, and he would make sure Ollis had what he wanted and that he enjoyed himself.

So even though Ollis felt uncomfortable, he decided to put on a little show. He needed to get naked, and while he could just strip and wait for Meyer to do the same, he could also do more. He already knew that Meyer wanted him, but he wanted him to be unable to keep his hands off him. He wanted that serious expression to vanish from Meyer's face.

Ollis's t-shirt was the next thing to go. He threw it on the floor along with the sweater, then realized he hadn't taken his shoes off yet. Thankfully, he was wearing sneakers, so he could easily toe them off.

The same couldn't be said for his socks. Ollis felt like an idiot, so he took them off as quickly as possible and kicked them into a corner.

There. That was better. He was still wearing his jeans, but he was pretty sure he could take those off in a somewhat seducing way.

He crawled onto the bed backward, staring at Meyer. Meyer's focus was on him, and Ollis could see his gaze flickering over his body. It made him feel sexy, which he hadn't expected. It was clear that Meyer wanted him, and Ollis loved that. He wanted Meyer just as much.

He grabbed one of the pillows and stacked it on top of the other before leaning against them. He was half sprawled, exposing his chest, praying it was what Meyer wanted. He unbuttoned his jeans and slowly lowered the zipper, wincing at how loud the sound was in the silent room. Meyer was still staring and not doing anything else, and Ollis started to wonder if maybe this was a mistake, but he noticed the bulge in Meyer's jeans.

He grinned. His boyfriend wanted this.

Ollis raised his hips and wiggled out of his jeans. Sliding them down his legs wasn't as sexy as he'd hoped, but with a little wiggling and pushing, he managed to get them off one foot, then the other. When he realized he still had his underwear on, he almost groaned, but that was when Meyer finally moved.

He chuckled and leaned over the bed, grabbing one of Ollis's calves. Ollis shivered at the touch. How could he already be so horny when they hadn't done anything yet? Hell, Meyer wasn't even naked.

Like Meyer, Ollis was hard, and in his case, it was obvious. The fabric of his underwear was struggling to keep his cock in, and there was a damp spot where the head rested. Ollis wanted to take them off, but it was clear that Meyer had other intentions.

He knelt on the bed between Ollis's legs and ran a hand up his thigh. His touch was light but firm, making Ollis shiver in anticipation.

What would Meyer do?

He raised Ollis's leg and pressed a kiss to his ankle. Ollis hadn't expected that, but he was eager to see where this would go.

The next kiss landed on his calf. Meyer moved higher with every kiss, and things got even more interesting when he added a scrape of teeth. It was enough to make Ollis want to beg for more, but before he could, Meyer looked up.

His eyes glittered. "Do you know that vampires don't always feed from the neck?"

Ollis's mouth was suddenly dry. "Don't they?"

Meyer shook his head and ran his fingertips up Ollis's inner thigh. "There are other places from which to feed. Of course, it depends on who they feed on, but between lovers, a favorite is a spot on the inner thigh. It's very sensitive, and many people appreciate it."

Ollis shuddered at the thought of Meyer feeding from his thigh. Had he been hesitant before? He couldn't even remember it. He wanted what Meyer was saying.

He looked at his lover and nodded. He hoped Meyer wouldn't make him say it, although he would if he had to. He just wasn't sure he could make the right words come out of his mouth.

Meyer grabbed the sides of Ollis's underwear and pulled. Ollis raised his hips to help him, groaning at the feeling of the fabric scraping down his body as it moved. He was fully naked in front of Meyer, and the fact that Meyer was still dressed was incredibly hot.

What Meyer did next was, too.

He grinned, showing Ollis his fangs, then leaned down to kiss Ollis's inner thigh. Ollis waited for the bite, but instead, he felt the press of lips. They ran up and down his thigh, coming dangerously close to his cock before retreating.

He wasn't sure what Meyer was trying to do, but if it was to drive him nuts, he was doing a great job. Ollis barely even realized when Meyer leaned sideways to open his nightstand. He was so focused on the sensations on his thigh that it took him a moment to realize that Meyer had taken out a bottle of lube.

This was it. They were about to make love.

Ollis couldn't wait.

But like everything else, Meyer seemed to want to take his time. He pressed closer to Ollis's body, his lips still playing on the skin of his inner thigh. He'd been right when he'd said the area was sensitive. Every one of his touches made Ollis want to scream, and he hadn't even gotten to Ollis's cock yet. What would happen when he did? Ollis suspected he'd see stars.

He watched Meyer open the lube, but his brain couldn't make sense of what was happening. He just knew that he wanted more, so he opened his legs wider. Meyer followed the movement, his lips never leaving Ollis's skin. Ollis almost asked him what he was waiting for, but he didn't have to.

Just as slick fingers touched his hole, Ollis felt Meyer's fangs sink into his thigh. He cried out, burying his fingers into Meyer's hair. He didn't know if he wanted to push Meyer away because the pleasure was too much or if he wanted to pull him close to have more.

The feeling of Meyer's fingers inside of him, of Meyer's fangs in his flesh, was something he wasn't sure he would ever get used to. It made him feel like he and Meyer were one, and the pleasure was like nothing he'd ever experienced. He could feel Meyer's lips move on his skin as he swallowed, but that was a secondary sensation next to the pleasure burning in his body.

He barely felt the invasion of Meyer's fingers inside of him. His entire focus was on his pleasure, and the fingers helped with that. Meyer clearly knew what he was doing as he prepped Ollis. He made sure to touch that sensitive spot deep inside of him repeatedly, driving Ollis closer to orgasm with every movement.

Ollis had no idea which way was up and which was down until he felt Meyer lick the bite on his thigh. He blinked, opening his mouth to ask what was happening, but Meyer was already moving.

He rose on his knees, but he didn't strip. He just unfastened his jeans, and Ollis watched him as he leaned closer. Meyer's cock was hard, and it was aimed right at Ollis.

Ollis grinned and hooked his legs around Meyer's, pulling him close. He wanted this, and there was no need for him to say it out loud. His body was doing the talking for him, and the sensation of Meyer's rough jeans against the skin of Ollis's legs was maddening and arousing at the same time. It made Ollis want to strip Meyer naked, but even more so, it made him want to beg Meyer to fuck him into the mattress.

Meyer entered him in one smooth movement that made Ollis cry out. He dug his fingers into Meyer's arms, holding on for dear life as Meyer started fucking him. There was no hesitation in the way Meyer moved. Ollis wanted Meyer to make him his, to possess him entirely. He wanted to feel owned but wouldn't have known how to ask for it.

Meyer seemed to know what Ollis needed. He never slowed down, never tried to turn it sweet. He just fucked all sense out of Ollis, and Ollis was there for it.

His cock was hard and leaked between their bodies, and he wondered if he could come without touching it. He was tempted to try but didn't want anything to ruin this moment. He reached for it, but Meyer leaned closer before he could touch it. Ollis watched him with wide eyes, wondering what came next.

Meyer buried his face against Ollis's neck and bit him. Ollis screamed as pleasure blasted through his body. He clung to Meyer as his cock jerked between them, not surprised to have come without having to touch it. Feeling Meyer's fangs again had been enough.

Meyer wrung out Ollis's pleasure from him as he drank. This time, it didn't last long, and when Ollis felt him lick the wound, he was kind of sorry. He realized that Meyer probably wanted to make sure he didn't take too much, though, so he didn't argue.

He wasn't sure he could have, since Meyer was still fucking him.

Ollis's body felt loose and heavy, so he was grateful when it didn't take Meyer long to come. When he did, he groaned and pressed his lips against Ollis's neck again. He didn't bite him this time, but he allowed Ollis to hold him through his orgasm.

For a moment, the only sound in the room was that of both of them panting. Ollis's mind had finally stopped spinning. He felt at peace with the world and with himself, safe as he was in Meyer's arms.

"Is it going to be like this every time?" he asked.

Meyer pressed a kiss to Ollis's neck. "Do you want it to be?"

"I'd be an idiot if I said no, but I don't know if I can survive it."

Meyer laughed. "I'll make sure you do. I have plans for you and need you alive and well."

Ollis liked the sound of that.

Chapter Five

Meyer couldn't look away from his phone. He already knew that nothing he'd see on the news would be good, but it was like a car crash. He needed to know what was happening. He needed more details to know where the dragons were attacking, how many casualties there were, and more. He felt useless, even with all that knowledge.

There was nothing he could do against the dragons. He was only one vampire, and while he was stronger than a human, he'd only end up dead if he tried to intervene. The problem was that no one was doing anything.

The dragons had started attacking more often. They were using blitz attacks, suddenly appearing, burning down buildings, and killing people before disappearing again. There hadn't been another attack like the one at the mall, but the number of deaths was still rising.

Meyer didn't understand what they were doing. Why did the alpha want to be feared? What did he think it would do? So far, the only thing that had happened was that the human government had sent the military. Unfortunately for them and everyone who lived in the area, it wasn't enough. Even with all their guns, men, and rockets, they weren't doing enough damage. It was as if the dragons knew what they'd do before they did it, and they escaped before anything happened—when they didn't fight back and win.

"I think they're targeting supernatural communities," Parker said.

He and Meyer were once again sitting by Luca's door.

Meyer had enough of this and thought it was ridiculous, and he had half a mind to talk to Kieran. He understood that the alpha had better things to do than talk to Luca, but Luca could help, and even if he couldn't, it would free two people from guarding his door twenty-four-seven. He hadn't tried anything, not even to escape. He wasn't dangerous, not to the pack and certainly not to Parker.

"They're targeting everyone in town," Meyer pointed out.

"Well, yeah, but I was wondering why they chose the areas they're attacking. Why there and not somewhere else?"

Meyer frowned. "Have you looked into it?"

"Luca and I talked about it. He grew up in the area, so he knows more than I do, and he confirmed that a lot of the buildings taken down by the clan housed supernatural people. Hell, there are so many of them without a home anymore that Kieran opened the pack to them. What does that tell you?"

Meyer got to his feet. He had nervous energy to burn before he headed out to pick up Ollis. He might as well pace the hallway as he thought about what Parker had said.

Kieran had started taking in refugees. With the dragons attacking more often, people were losing their homes. The pack had many members, but most of the supernatural communities in town were much smaller. No matter how hard their alphas tried, they couldn't take care of their people, especially when they themselves had lost everything.

Meyer was glad that Kieran had opened his territory to them, but he couldn't help but wonder if that didn't make them an even bigger target. Many supernatural creatures were gathering in pack territory. The dragons knew where the pack lived, so what were they waiting for? Why hadn't they attacked yet? Were they waiting for even more people to move here?

If they were, they'd only have to strike once. The thought

made Meyer shudder in horror, but once again, there was nothing he could do.

"Even if they *are* targeting supernatural creatures, what can we do about it?" he asked.

Parker looked crestfallen. "I guess everyone already knows to be careful. You're right, it doesn't change anything."

"I don't know about that. I just wonder what their goal is. Are they trying to kill every supernatural creature in the area? Why would they do that?"

"Because most of them want nothing to do with the clan," Luca said from behind his bedroom door.

Talking to him without seeing him was infuriating, and Meyer had had enough. He looked from the door to Parker, then back at the door. The key hung from a hook on the wall and was only used to give Luca food.

That was over now. Meyer wasn't going to allow Luca to leave the bedroom until Kieran approved, but he could open the door. If Luca had wanted to attack them or escape, he would have done so a while ago. Instead, he was still here, sitting on his bed all day, every day. It had to be mind-numbingly boring, but he hadn't complained once.

Meyer grabbed the key. He didn't stop to look at Parker, but his brother grabbed his arm. "What are you doing?"

"I don't know about you, but I've had enough of talking to him through the door."

"What if Kieran finds out?"

"I'll explain my reasoning. I don't care, Parker. He might be able to help us, but we're not allowing him to try. What if he's the only person who can save the pack?"

"You have too much faith in me," Luca said.

Meyer didn't think Luca could solve their problems with the clan by himself, but Kieran kept saying they needed all the allies they could find. That had to include Luca, right?

Meyer unlocked the door and opened it. Luca had stepped

aside and was standing in the middle of the bedroom, a frown on his face. He eyed Meyer warily as if he expected Meyer to hurt him, but Meyer slapped the key back into place.

"What were you saying?" he asked.

Luca hesitated, then went to sit on his bed. He didn't even try to get close to the door, which confirmed that he wasn't planning to escape. Meyer hadn't thought he was. Something was growing between Luca and Parker, and he suspected that Luca wanted to stay for that reason—and probably because he didn't have anywhere else to go.

"The way the alpha sees it, you're with the clan or you die," Luca explained. "The problem is that you can only be with the clan if you're a dragon shifter. He doesn't accept anyone else. In fact, he never accepts anyone into the clan. You're either born in it or not. You can't become a clan member like you all became pack members. That means everyone else out there who might create trouble for the clan must die."

"Why would he think these people could create trouble? He's been targeting smaller groups. I doubt any of them had plans to attack the clan." Even the pack couldn't, and they were one of the biggest shifter groups in the area.

"Maybe they can't do much by themselves, but Kieran is trying to gather everyone. What would happen if the clan had to face not only the pack but also a bunch of other people? Even if Kieran only manages to convince, say, two manticore shifters, that will still be two manticore shifters who could attack the clan."

Meyer supposed it made sense. If Kieran gathered enough people, they could defeat the clan. It wouldn't be easy, and there would be many losses, but they didn't have a choice. It was either them or the dragons.

The dragon alpha knew that. He was taking out the people he believed would rise against him before they could attempt it. He was trying to isolate Kieran and the pack, possibly hoping that the pack wouldn't fight back when he attacked. Meyer could have told him it was ridiculous and that the wolves would never stop defending their home, but he suspected that wasn't something this alpha could understand. He saw his people as puppets, and he was focused on his own wealth and power. He wouldn't understand how Kieran could care about his people and be ready to lose every single inch of pack territory if it meant saving more of them.

Meyer didn't know if this would be of any help, but it was one step forward to understanding how the dragon alpha thought. Hopefully, it would help them anticipate what he was planning next so they could step in before more people got hurt.

It might not be enough, but it was something.

"I'll talk to Kieran when I see him later," Meyer said. "I don't know if he's realized this, but if he hasn't, he will."

Luca nodded. "I'm sorry I can't help any more than that."

"It's better than nothing." Meyer eyed him. "Are you going to try to escape?"

Luca shook his head. "I don't have a reason to."

That was what Meyer had suspected, and while he wanted more details, he didn't need them.

Luca was staying because he wanted to. A bedroom door wouldn't be enough to keep a dragon shifter prisoner, and Meyer would make sure to point that out to Kieran, too. Luca was here because he wanted to be and wasn't going anywhere.

They might as well use him.

"Thank you for bringing this to my attention. I'll mention it to Kieran and see what he thinks of it, but I don't think there should be any problems," Ollis said as he guided the woman he'd been talking to toward the door.

He didn't love the fact that he had to see people at his home. He hadn't thought about it before, since Kieran didn't seem to be bothered by it, but Ollis didn't have a nice office. He'd never needed one, and he'd had to improvise. He was meeting people in his kitchen over a cup of coffee, and they seemed to like it, but he could tell some of them were wary. They didn't know what to expect from him and weren't sure he'd be a good substitute for Kieran.

He was doing his best. He hadn't had to make any massive decision yet, and he hoped that wouldn't change. He talked things through with Kieran and Sloan every night, and they seemed to believe he was doing a good job, so they left the decisions to him.

It was terrifying. Ollis hadn't expected how scary it would be to make decisions for so many people, and he didn't know if he'd ever get used to it. Thankfully, he wouldn't have to. Eventually, this war would be over, and Kieran would be in charge again. Ollis could go back to his normal life of being a guard for the pack and dating Meyer.

"Thank you for hearing me out," Mrs. Benson said.

"I'm always here whenever you need me," Ollis promised.

"I wasn't sure what to think of this before, but you seem like a good man. Everyone's worried about what the dragons are doing."

"That's why Kieran needed more help. He's focused on keeping the pack safe, and he'll do it. I have faith in him."

Mrs. Benson nodded as they reached Ollis's front door. "I do, too. What the dragons are doing is awful. Someone needs to stop them."

Ollis hoped that someone would be Kieran, but there was no way to tell. No matter how many allies Kieran found, the possibility that the dragons would win was still high.

But that wasn't something Ollis was supposed to worry about. He did, but he couldn't do anything about it, and he was glad. It was complicated enough to deal with the everyday bickering between pack members and the many problems every pack had.

He opened the door to let Mrs. Benson out. "I should have an answer for you soon. It's unfortunate that the dragons destroyed your store, and of course, the pack will help you rebuild. I'm afraid it's going to have to wait until the dragons have been dealt with, but it's on the list."

"I'm willing to wait however long it takes. I suspect that if we were to start rebuilding now, the dragons would target the store again. I was lucky my granddaughter was sick that day, so I wasn't working."

The dragons seemed to be targeting stores and houses owned by supernatural creatures. It wasn't just the pack but a wide range of people. Kieran had needed to take in some of the people who'd lost everything, even though they weren't pack members. They needed a place to stay, and he'd opened pack territory to them. Ollis thought it was a good thing, but he'd heard a few people grumbling about it.

Mrs. Benson left, and Ollis closed the door behind her. He rested against it for a moment, closing his eyes and thinking about the work he'd done today.

He couldn't believe he was doing this. Most people who mattered to him had told him they believed in him, but he hadn't been sure he'd do a good job. He'd been terrified and still was, but he thought it was going well. Even though some people didn't trust him, he felt like most of the pack had enough faith in him to believe he'd do what was best for them. They didn't hesitate to bring him their problems, which was what he was here for.

Thankfully, his day was almost over. He only had his meeting with Kieran to get through. Then he could dive into his bed and sleep for the next eight hours. He might even be able to convince Meyer to spend the night with him.

Ollis went upstairs to shower and dress. He felt he needed more coffee, but if he drank more, he suspected he'd have a hard time falling asleep. He was tempted, so he was relieved when a knock on the door interrupted him before he could make that mistake.

It had to be Meyer, since Ollis had been clear that he wouldn't see anyone after seven in the evening. He needed a little time to relax before he saw Kieran, and he'd met so many people today that his mind spun. He was taking notes so he wouldn't make a mess of everyone's problems, but it was still a lot when he wasn't used to any of this.

As a guard, he'd spent most of his time in the forest, both as a human and a wolf. He was often assigned to patrol with a partner, but it wasn't comparable to what he'd done these past few days.

He opened the door, happy to see Meyer, only to freeze.

It wasn't Meyer. It was Malcolm.

"Don't slam the door in my face," Malcolm quickly said.

"That's what you deserve."

Ollis expected Malcolm to brush off his words and make a joke, but instead, his brother nodded. "You're right. I do deserve for you not to listen to me. What I did to you was awful, and I hate that I didn't realize it sooner."

Ollis blinked, sure he'd heard that wrong. "What are you talking about?"

Malcolm looked around as if he expected someone to hear them talking. He'd probably be more comfortable inside, but there was no way Ollis would let him in. If Malcolm was going to apologize, he could do it on the porch.

"I guess I got used to teasing you when we were younger. Back then, I never thought much of it. I was an asshole, and you're my younger brother. Of course I thought you were immature and stupid. The teasing should've stopped when we grew up, but I've always seen you as my little brother. I never actually stopped to look at what you're doing with your life, especially recently. I guess I was used to the idea of you being irresponsible and immature, and I didn't see that you'd grown up and had become an adult. You're not a kid anymore, and neither am I, even though I remained stuck in a teenager mentality."

Ollis gaped. He'd thought Malcolm would mope around for a bit, then behave as if nothing had happened. He could never have imagined that his brother would apologize to him and admit how wrong he'd been.

Yet here they were.

Malcolm rubbed the back of his neck. "So again, I'm sorry. You might always be my younger brother, but you're not so little anymore, and I have to accept that. I'll stop behaving like an asshole. You grew up more than I ever did, but it's time I caught up."

Ollis couldn't help being suspicious. "Why now? What changed that you finally see what you're doing?"

"In part, it was Kieran choosing you. I never expected him to choose me for something like this, and frankly, I'm glad he didn't, but I also didn't expect him to choose *you*. He saw you as you truly are, unlike me. No matter how frightened I am by what the dragons are doing, I trust Kieran to keep us safe. That means I have to trust his choice when it comes to you, too."

It made sense, but he didn't feel like enough. "I have a hard time believing you managed to get your head out of your ass by yourself."

Malcolm grimaced. "Mom and Dad talked to me, and Heather made sure I knew what she thought of my behavior after the meeting at the community center. She didn't mince her words."

"So it took your wife to make you see it?"

"I think before, I didn't *want* to see it. Life was easier when nothing changed, including you. But things *are* changing, and I have to accept that, because otherwise I'll start losing people I care about, including you."

Ollis would never have expected his brother to do this, but he was glad he was. He didn't want to lose any member of his family, especially not during such dangerous times. He wasn't sure he could forgive Malcolm, but he could start healing, and that was what mattered the most.

Meyer tensed when he reached Ollis's house and saw him talking to someone on the porch. It took him a moment to recognize the person, and when he did, he told himself to take things slow. Ollis and Malcolm weren't fighting. They were talking, and both appeared calm. Meyer couldn't go off on Malcolm the way he had at the community center.

He wondered if he should stay in the forest for a bit longer and give the brothers time to talk things out, but he stepped on something that cracked, and Ollis looked up. His smile told Meyer that he wanted him there, so he walked out of the woods and toward his boyfriend's house.

Malcolm turned to see who was coming and tensed. Meyer arched a brow, silently daring him to say something about his presence. When Malcolm thought his brother was immature and useless, he'd believed that Meyer wasn't a good enough boyfriend. Did he still feel the same? Meyer hoped that his presence here meant that the brothers were making up, which in turn might mean that Malcolm had a problem with him. If he hadn't thought Meyer was good enough for his brother before, he certainly wouldn't think he was good enough now.

Malcolm nodded at Meyer when he reached them. "I was just leaving."

Ollis looked amused. "He's not going to drink you dry, you know," he told his brother. "If he were to drink from someone, it'd be me."

Malcolm's eyes widened. "You let him drink from you?"

"Why? You have something against that?"

Malcolm's jaw tightened, and Meyer could see how torn he was in his expression. It looked like he and Ollis had been talking things through, and Malcolm clearly didn't want to jeopardize that. He clearly also didn't want Meyer to be involved with Ollis, so this might be a problem.

"I don't," Malcolm said. "What you do with your boyfriend is not my business. You're an adult."

Meyer did his best not to look impressed. He hadn't expected Malcolm to be so reasonable. Malcolm had pitched a fit the last time they'd been here.

"Thank you," Ollis said. "I'll talk to you tomorrow. Meyer and I have to go and see Kieran."

"All right. Sorry if I kept you."

"You didn't."

Malcolm paused and nodded at Meyer again before scurrying off the porch.

Meyer was surprised he wasn't running. He wanted to tease Malcolm about not drinking from him again, but he could see genuine fear in the man.

Maybe that was why he'd reacted the way he had when Ollis had told him he and Meyer were together. Maybe it wasn't just that he didn't think Ollis was mature enough to make the decision to be with a vampire. He might have been afraid for his brother, and that was something Meyer could understand.

Many wolf shifters were wary of vampires because they barely knew anything about them. If Malcolm was fearful for his brother, Meyer could excuse his behavior, at least when it came to him.

Ollis stepped forward and pushed into Meyer's arms. Meyer wrapped them around him, able to tell that his boyfriend needed comfort.

"Everything okay?" he asked as he kissed the tip of Ollis's head.

"Yeah. I talked to a lot of people today, and I didn't expect Malcolm to come around."

"I'm surprised he came to apologize."

"I was, too. I wasn't sure what to expect when I found him on my porch, but he seems to truly regret what he did."

"Are you going to give him another chance?"

"Yeah. People are losing enough loved ones because of the dragons. It would be stupid to lose my brother just because I'm too proud to accept his apology. I'm not saying our relationship will be perfect. We have to work on it, and it won't be easy, but I think that in the end, I'd regret it if I didn't give him another chance."

That meant that Meyer would have to give Malcolm another chance, too. He wasn't happy about it, but he'd do it if Ollis needed it. He wanted Ollis to be happy, which apparently meant having a relationship with his brother.

Meyer could understand that. Sometimes, his siblings were infuriating, but he loved them too much to allow their relationship to crumble. Even when they fought, they always talked things through and made peace. Ollis was right. Too many people were dying and losing everything. The rest of them needed to be united.

He kissed Ollis's hair again. "Ready to go?"

"Ready to go to bed, but we have to talk to Kieran first," Ollis complained.

"You can go to bed as soon as we're back," Meyer promised.

"You don't want to spend the night at your house?"

They'd taken to the habit of spending the night there. That first time, Meyer suspected that Ollis had wanted to stay away from his house in case his brother tried to find him. He hadn't wanted to talk to him about what happened during the pack meeting, and Meyer couldn't blame him for that. Malcolm had been an asshole, so why would Ollis have wanted to talk to him?

It had become a habit, maybe because Ollis was meeting the pack at his home and wanted to separate that part of his life from his private life. It was a pity that he felt he wasn't fully at home in his house, and Meyer hoped that would change. He loved his family and didn't mind living with them, but it was a lot of people to share a home with, especially when he wanted privacy with Ollis. At the same time, Ollis was safer with all of them around, so Meyer was torn.

They headed out. The path between Ollis's house and Kieran's was becoming familiar, which pleased Meyer. When he'd agreed to move into pack territory and help, he hadn't expected to want to permanently move here. He wasn't entirely sure how to deal with it, but he and Ollis were taking things at a pace they were comfortable with. Meyer didn't care if it was too fast or too slow. He just cared that they were both satisfied with it, especially Ollis.

He was so much younger than Meyer. Most people were, since Meyer was a vampire, and it took some time getting used to. When Meyer had relationships in the past, they had always been with other vampires. He'd had flings with humans and other supernatural creatures but felt more comfortable with people who understood his immortality.

He wasn't sure Ollis did. There were many things Meyer didn't want to think about when it came to their future, so he hadn't brought it up, and he wasn't planning on doing so anytime soon. Ollis would think about it eventually, but they had the dragons to focus on right now. Once that was over, they'd have time to worry about everything else.

He listened to Ollis as he talked about the people he'd met with today. Ollis had been worried he wouldn't do a good job, but Meyer could tell from listening to him that he cared about the people who came to him. He was passionate about helping his pack in any way he could, and he never hesitated to ask for help when he felt he wasn't up to the task. He took people seriously, even when their problems could seem trivial to someone else.

Meyer couldn't have resisted falling in love with him even if he'd tried.

When they reached Kieran's house, Meyer stopped Ollis before he could knock. Ollis turned to him, and Meyer leaned down to kiss him. He felt Ollis smile against his lips, and even though he had to keep the kiss short, it felt like an eternity.

"What was that for?" Ollis asked.

"Just because. You're incredible."

"Doesn't feel like a good enough reason, but I'll take it."

Eventually, Ollis would believe he was enough. Meyer would make sure of it.

Ollis was still focused on Meyer when the door opened. He hadn't knocked, but Robin had been expecting them. Kieran had agreed to have Ollis around every evening so they could talk about his day until he felt more comfortable with the decisions he needed to make. Ollis wasn't sure he ever would, and he was glad to be able to talk to his alpha.

Robin looked exhausted. He gestured at Meyer and Ollis to come in. Ollis kept an eye on Robin, wondering what he could do to help. "Do you need anything?"

Robin blinked as if surprised that Ollis was asking. "No, thank you. I just spent several hours on the phone with someone."

Ollis blinked. "When you were supposed to be asleep?"

"Not everyone remembers that as a vampire, I'm supposed to sleep during the day. Others do remember but are displeased about talking to a vampire, so they ignore it or do it on purpose."

Ollis gritted his teeth. "Do we *want* these people to be our allies?"

"Normally, I'd say no, but we need everyone we can find."

Unfortunately, Robin was right. They did need everyone they could convince to help them in this war, and that included assholes who didn't like vampires.

"Kieran is waiting for you," Robin said as he gestured toward the office.

Ollis squeezed his shoulder as he walked past him. He wished he could do more for Robin and everyone else, but he was already shouldering a heavy load of work. Taking on more would exhaust him, and he wouldn't be able to help when they most needed him to.

He and Meyer got to the office only to find that Kieran was in pretty much the same state as Robin. It looked like he might put his head down on his desk and fall asleep right there, and Ollis decided that he'd keep this short. He should probably stop coming here every night. He still felt like he needed it, but it was clear that Kieran couldn't deal with it anymore.

"We can go if you want," he offered.

Kieran shook his head. "I need at least a few minutes with friends. This day has been hell."

"Robin mentioned it."

Kieran rubbed his eyes. "I should have remembered that alphas are usually assholes. Dealing with them makes me want to scream."

"I'll be quick, then. There's not much to worry about. I've had a few requests for help, mostly for things I can deal with myself, but there are a few things you need to weigh in on. Mrs. Benson had her store destroyed during one of the attacks, and she wants help to rebuild. I told her it shouldn't be a problem but that she'd have to wait."

"That sounds perfect. What did she say?"

"She was fine with it. Most people are when I tell them what I've decided."

Ollis was still surprised. He'd expected people to argue and try to get him to change his mind, then throw a tantrum and go find Kieran. They seemed to realize how important Kieran's work was, though, and mostly, they left him alone. Ollis wouldn't go as far as to say that everyone trusted him, but they at least seemed to respect him.

"It's good to hear that the pack has my back. Unfortunately, I can't say the same for anyone else," Kieran said.

"Has someone in particular been giving you problems?" Meyer asked.

"Some of the alphas want us to jump through hoops so much that it sounds like they don't truly want to help. I don't understand why. Shouldn't they want the dragons to be taken care of? I don't know how they don't see that the clan will turn to them as soon as they're done with us."

"I suppose that some of them hope the clan will either ignore them or ask them to be on their side," Ollis offered.

Meyer snorted. "To hear Luca, they won't have much luck."

Kieran looked hesitant. "I know what he told you, but he might be wrong."

"I doubt it. He knows the dragons better than anyone here. He was adamant that the alpha won't ever welcome anyone into the clan, and I believe him."

Ollis had been there for the conversation between Meyer and Kieran. Meyer had insisted that Luca needed to be allowed out of his bedroom, and while Kieran had been wary, he'd eventually agreed. As long as Luca stayed in the house where the vampires lived, he could leave his bedroom cell.

Ollis had seen him several times since then. Luca was always with Parker, one of Meyer's brothers. Every time Ollis said something about it, Meyer shook his head as if disappointed. Maybe he was, but Ollis didn't see a problem with Parker and Luca being together.

Like Meyer, he trusted Luca to want the same thing they did. He'd left his clan because he disagreed with what they did, as would anyone in their right mind. No matter why everyone else stayed behind, Luca had found the courage not to. It was impressive, and while it would take time for people to trust him, he could see Luca becoming a pack member somewhere down the line. He'd have to prove himself during the fight with his clan, but if he'd left the clan for the right reasons, Ollis was sure he'd be on their side.

Meyer's phone rang. He took it out, his eyes widening when he saw the screen. Kieran and Ollis exchanged a glance, but Meyer didn't tell them who it was before answering.

"Alice," he said. "I thought you'd forgotten about me."

Ollis leaned closer to hear the other side of the conversation. Meyer had told him about his hydra shifter friend, so he recognized her name.

"It's you who always forgets about me, not the other way around," she teased. "I talked to Carla and wanted to let you know as soon as possible."

"Wait a moment. I'm with my alpha, and he'll want to hear this." Meyer lowered his phone and put it on speaker. "Go ahead. Kieran is listening."

"Alpha," Alice said. "It's a pleasure to meet you, although I wish it were in better circumstances."

"I believe we share that wish," Kieran said. "Meyer told me he contacted you for help. We sorely need it, unfortunately."

"I talked to my sister, who's the alpha of our clan. She agrees that the dragons need to be stopped and that they've done enough harm, but she'd like to meet you and your people first."

Ollis and Meyer looked at each other. Ollis had known this

might happen, and he was prepared for it, but it was still terrifying.

"Would you like to visit our territory?" Kieran suggested.

"No offense, but I don't think that's a good idea. If the dragons decide to attack you while we're there, our clan will lose their alpha and their beta. We should meet in a neutral location, maybe halfway between our territories."

"I agree. Tell me when and where, and I'll be there."

"We'd like to meet your beta, too. Meyer didn't tell me much, but I know you have a partner who can take care of the clan if you're both absent. My sister's husband will stay behind."

Ollis swallowed. Robin might stay, just in case, but he wouldn't be the one in charge. That would be Ollis. It would be the first time he had to lead the pack on his own, and while he hoped Kieran wouldn't be gone for long, this was what Kieran had asked him to do. More importantly, it was what Kieran *needed* him to do, and Ollis had sworn to help him in any way he could. No matter how scared he was, he'd do it.

He'd be fine. Even with Kieran and Sloan gone, Ollis wouldn't be on his own. Meyer would be there, along with Robin and Meyer's family. Even Malcolm was on Ollis's side now.

Besides, what would be the odds of something happening the first time Kieran left?

Chapter Six

Meyer looked at the group gathered in front of the house. He'd expected Merrick to stay behind. They'd need the dragon if the clan decided to attack. Unfortunately, Merrick decided to go with Kieran. He didn't trust Alice and Carla, but then, he didn't trust anyone. It made sense that he wanted to protect Kieran, but it left Meyer worried. Arlen and Luca would be staying, but a third dragon shifter could make the difference between winning and losing if the dragons attacked.

Maybe the clan wouldn't attack. How would they know that Kieran and Sloan were gone? Unless they had a spy, they couldn't, which meant they couldn't take advantage of it.

If they *did* have a spy, it wasn't Luca. He didn't know that both Kieran and Sloan would be gone today. He didn't know what was happening because he wasn't allowed to leave the house, and everyone made sure not to talk about anything important in front of him.

At least he wasn't locked in his bedroom anymore. It felt odd to talk to him face-to-face, but he and Parker were like two peas in a pod, and Meyer doubted that would change anytime soon. Meyer might as well get used to having Luca in his life. Hopefully, the dragon wouldn't hurt Parker.

"Call if you need anything," Kieran told Ollis.

Ollis was pale and a bit shaky, but he was doing his best to appear strong. Meyer was proud of him and wanted to remind him that he wouldn't be alone even though Kieran was leaving. Everyone was on edge because, with the alpha gone, the pack would be more vulnerable, but that didn't mean they'd be open to an attack.

Of course, if the clan attacked, there was little they could do, even if Kieran was here. They couldn't face a bunch of angry dragon shifters and win. That was why Kieran was trying to find allies. Meyer had wanted to be at the meeting, if anything to see Alice, but Ollis was staying behind, which meant that Meyer was, too. He'd explained to Alice why he wouldn't be there, and she'd understood. Besides, Meyer hoped that she and Carla would soon be coming to pack territory. If they were going to fight the dragons with the pack, they'd have to.

"I won't need anything," Ollis promised. "You need to focus on your meeting and not worry about what I'm doing. I promise I have everything in hand."

"I know. I wouldn't have chosen you if I didn't believe that."

Ollis was still flustered when Kieran said things like that, but Meyer thought he'd come to accept that no matter how the rest of the world saw him, Kieran saw the real him. He was a grown man, a hard worker, and he cared so fucking much. It would destroy him if anything happened to the pack on his watch, which was one of the reasons he was so tense.

Kieran and the others quickly climbed into their vehicles. Robin looked like he wanted to jump into the one where Kieran was, but they'd both decided it would be best for him to stay back because the pack needed to see him since both the alpha and the beta were leaving. Meyer could understand why Robin was so nervous, and he felt lucky that no one cared if he stayed with Ollis.

"Something tells me this is going to be a disaster," Ollis murmured as he and Meyer watched the cars drive away.

Meyer hooked an arm around his boyfriend's shoulders. "It won't be. You know what you're doing."

"I do, but what about the dragons?"

"They're waiting for something, and I don't think that something is Kieran leaving. When they do attack, they'll want to take out all of us simultaneously. They won't want to leave anyone who can give them trouble behind, especially Kieran."

The corner of Ollis's lips curled. "So you're saying they think Kieran is trouble?"

"I'm sure they do. They wouldn't have targeted the pack otherwise." But Meyer was still worried. He didn't want to burden Ollis, but he couldn't stop thinking.

What if the clan decided to take out the substitute alpha? With Ollis gone, they could take over the pack and wait for Kieran to come back. Ollis and Kieran had agreed that Ollis would call Kieran tonight and tomorrow before he and the others came back, but would it be enough? What if the clan attacked in the meantime?

There was no way to find out what they'd do, unfortunately.

Ollis sighed. "Well, the only thing I can do now is my job. I'm going to go home so I can start seeing the people who have appointments with me."

"You're not going anywhere," Meyer told him.

Ollis blinked. "What are you talking about?"

"Text the people you're supposed to see and tell them to come over to the house where my family lives. I don't want you alone, especially in the middle of the forest. I love your house, but it's too isolated and too far away for anyone to reach it quickly if something happens."

Ollis looked like he wanted to argue, but thankfully, he didn't. He had to realize it was for the best if they stuck together.

"Some of these people aren't going to be happy to have to come to your house," he warned.

"I don't care. If they don't want to come, they'll have to

schedule a new appointment with you. I need you close to me and my family. We'll protect you if anything happens."

Meyer led the way toward the house while Ollis texted a few people and called others. From the sound of it, everyone agreed to meet him at Meyer's house, and while there were a few grumbles, they seemed to understand how important this was. Even if they didn't, Ollis was technically their alpha, which meant that what he said went. If he wanted to meet them in the middle of the woods, that was where he'd meet them.

Thankfully, they weren't headed to the middle of the woods. They reached the house quickly, and Meyer ushered Ollis inside. Tyrian came out of the living room as Meyer closed the door. He didn't seem surprised to see Ollis, and he gestured at him to follow. "We set up the office," he said.

Ollis looked at him with wide eyes. "Why?"

"Because I suspected you'd be staying here. Hopefully, it won't be long before Kieran comes back, but in the meantime, we all agree it's safer for you to be here."

Meyer squeezed Ollis's shoulder. "We talked about it, and you're welcome here."

Tyrian smiled. "And not only because you're our alpha. You're Meyer's partner, and that means a lot to us."

Ollis appeared overwhelmed, so Meyer gently guided him toward the office. They hadn't set it up until now because they hadn't needed it. The office could be Ollis's until Kieran got back.

Meyer let his father take Ollis to the office. He wanted the two of them to become closer, and it was a good idea for them to spend time together. Tyrian wasn't an alpha, but he'd been the leader of their family for hundreds of years. He knew something about being a figure of authority and how to deal with the problems that came with that. He'd support Ollis until Kieran came back, which was one of the reasons Meyer had wanted Ollis here.

There was no one Meyer trusted more than his father to keep Ollis safe and to help him. It made him feel better about their messy situation, and he knew that even if he wasn't there, Ollis would never be unprotected.

Meyer's family would keep an eye on Ollis, as they should. Meyer wouldn't hesitate to protect Madison if Tyrian wasn't there. Hell, he'd even protect Luca since he was important to Parker. Luca wasn't an official part of their family yet, but Meyer had no doubt that he would be eventually. He still wasn't quite sure how he felt about it, but he was willing to give Luca a chance. As long as he made Parker happy and treated him right, everyone would.

But Luca wasn't what Meyer was the most worried about. He was worried about the dragons, and part of him couldn't help but wonder if they'd take this opportunity to attack.

He wasn't sure the pack would be ready if they did.

Ollis was relieved that Meyer had insisted he come home with him. He could have gone to his house, and he'd planned on doing just that, but the thought of being alone there had made him nervous.

He expected something to go wrong. He hadn't told anyone because he wanted to look like he knew what he was doing, but he couldn't shake the feeling that something was about to happen. Sloan and Kieran were away from the pack, which would be the best moment for someone to attack. Even if they knew Ollis had been put in charge, they'd probably expect him not to know what he was doing or not to be as good an alpha as Kieran. Ollis couldn't say he'd blame them. No matter how seriously he took it, he could never be half the alpha Kieran was. He didn't believe alphas should all come from the same families or anything like that. He'd just never wanted to be one, and he still didn't.

The weight of the responsibilities was so heavy that sometimes when he paused to think about it, he felt he couldn't breathe. Right now, *he* was responsible for his pack. He was making decisions for all pack members. If something happened, he'd be in charge of keeping them safe.

He wasn't sure he could.

He'd do his best, but would his best be enough? If the dragons attacked, it wouldn't be. No matter how hard he fought, they'd win.

He couldn't think about that right now. He had meetings to reorganize and people to talk to. Hopefully, by the time his long list of things to do was fulfilled, Kieran would be back. He'd planned to be away one night, but Ollis hoped it wouldn't take that long. If the hydra shifters got the answers they sought, they might not need to talk to Kieran for long. The sooner Kieran was back, the better it would be, and not only for Ollis. The entire pack would be safer if Kieran was here.

"I wouldn't worry too much if I were you," Meyer's father said as he showed Ollis the office.

Ollis couldn't believe they'd set it up for him. He hadn't expected it, and it made him feel emotional. Did it mean they accepted him as Meyer's partner? Unlike Ollis's brother, they didn't have a problem with Baxter dating Sloan. As soon as they'd realized that Meyer and Ollis were together, they'd behaved as if it was normal and expected. Meyer hadn't needed to talk to them or to explain anything. He'd told his family that he and Ollis were together, and that had been it.

It felt good to have that kind of support. Ollis's parents supported him, and now, so did Malcolm, but it didn't feel the same. The pack was all Ollis's family had ever known, but Meyer's family had seen what the world had to offer. They'd lived so much longer than Ollis could ever dream of, and it was overwhelming to think about, but Ollis also hoped that since they liked him, it meant he was a good person.

"I hope the office will be good enough for what you need to do," Tyrian continued. "We didn't have a lot of time to set it up. We just cleaned it and hoped for the best."

"It's perfect. I don't even have an office at home, so I meet people in my kitchen. This is too much, really."

Tyrian's smile was gentle. "It's not. Even if you and Meyer weren't together, I'd want to do this for you. You're doing a good job, Ollis, and I know you're worried, but you shouldn't be."

"Are you going to tell me no one will attack us while Kieran is away?"

"I wish I could, but I think we both know it would be a lie. The chances that someone will attack are high. I just meant that even if we *are* attacked, you won't face this alone. You have Meyer, the rest of our family, and most of the pack. They trust Kieran, so they trust you because he chose you."

"Sometimes, it feels like he made a mistake. What if I make the wrong decision?"

"You could," Tyrian admitted. "But what's the one thing you want the most?"

"To keep the pack safe." Ollis didn't have to think about it. Everyone he cared about was a pack member. He'd grown up here, and this would always be his home.

Tyrian nodded as if he expected that answer. "Exactly. You'll do everything you can to save the pack, which means you'll make the right decisions. Besides, I'm here. I'm not Kieran, but I know one or two things about guiding a group of people."

It wasn't the same, but Ollis supposed that Tyrian had experience when it came to that. He'd been guiding his family for hundreds of years, and sometimes, it looked like herding cats. Ollis would rather deal with the entire pack than with

Alpin.

Tyrian squeezed Ollis's shoulder. "Why don't you settle in? When should your first appointment arrive?"

Ollis checked the time on his phone. "In ten minutes."

Thankfully, everyone had agreed to come here. Ollis's place was more out of the way, so he guessed that even though some people didn't want to see vampires, it was better for them not to have to traipse all over the forest. Besides, he hadn't given anyone a choice. He'd been honest that he needed to be closer to where most of the pack lived in case something happened. A few people had argued, but he hadn't had to reschedule with anyone.

He wished he could have. He didn't know how he'd be able to focus on his meetings, but he was going to have to.

Luckily for Ollis, Tyrian kept things smooth and running quickly. It took Ollis a while to realize he'd taken it upon himself to be Ollis's personal assistant. He brought in Ollis's appointments, and he'd already scheduled another meeting for the two of them to catch up later in the month. When Ollis had tried telling him he could go, he'd waved at him and had told him it was a distraction he welcomed.

Ollis hadn't known what to say to that. He had no idea how old Tyrian was, but he'd lived hundreds of years. Ollis could imagine he'd be bored after a couple of hundred years, so maybe Tyrian was doing this for that reason. Maybe he *wanted* a distraction.

Ollis was happy to give him one.

He'd left his phone on the desk, and when he saw the screen light up right after Mr. West left, he quickly snatched it up. He frowned at the name of one of the guards on his screen. It had to be bad news. Why would a guard call him otherwise?

"Yes?" he asked when he answered.

"We're under attack!" the guard yelled.

Ollis bolted out of his chair. "Where? Who's attacking?"

"By the small dirt road. I think they used it to get here without anyone noticing."

Ollis swore. Only someone familiar with pack territory would know about that road. It was a back entrance that was seldom used. Pack members either drove in and out of pack territory through the main and better-maintained entrance or ran around in their wolf form. They didn't need to park on a small dirt road that turned to mud every time it rained.

"Who?" Ollis asked as someone on the guard's side of the conversation screamed.

"Wolves," the guard said before another scream made Ollis's ears ring.

He almost dropped the phone as he rushed out of the office. "Can you hear me?" he asked.

The guard didn't answer. No matter how many times he called out, he got no answer, but he could still hear the sound of a fight.

Ollis rushed into the kitchen. "We have to go," he said, not even checking who was there. "The pack is under attack."

Meyer's family surrounded Ollis in seconds. "Just tell us where, and we'll be there," one of Meyer's sisters said.

A hand landed on Ollis's shoulder, and he almost cried when he saw Meyer. He didn't want either of them to have to fight, but they didn't have a choice. Ollis couldn't hide in this house like he wanted to. He had to go out there and be an alpha.

Even though, at the moment, he felt nothing like one.

Meyer wished he could do more for Ollis, but he wasn't in charge. Ollis was, which meant he'd be the one giving the orders. Thankfully, they'd planned for something like this. Ollis just needed to be reminded that he knew what to do.

"Remember the plan," Meyer said.

Ollis stared at him. He looked lost, which was understandable. Meyer didn't feel the same, but he *was* terrified.

What if something happened to Ollis? What if the time they'd had together was coming to an end?

Meyer couldn't think about that. He had to focus on keeping the pack and Ollis safe, and he'd do it. He didn't have a choice.

Ollis shook himself. "I just got a call from one of the guards. He said we're under attack at the small dirt road. He also told me the attackers were wolves, which makes sense, because they'd know about that road."

Meyer felt better. He would have fought hard against dragons, but there would have been little he could have done to win. Wolves, on the other hand? Meyer had beaten wolf shifters' asses many times over his long life. He could do it again.

He would.

"Let's go," he said, gesturing at his family.

He wanted to stay behind and force Ollis to do the same. He wanted them to hide in the house while everyone else went out there and protected Ollis. Unfortunately, Ollis had refused that option when they'd talked about it. He'd said that as the alpha—even a temporary one—his place would be with the people fighting, and he wasn't wrong.

Meyer just wished he were.

Now that he'd gotten over the shock, Ollis seemed more comfortable taking charge. He led everyone outside, but once there, he hesitated and turned to Meyer. "I'm going to shift," he said as he started stripping, not caring one bit that he was in front of Meyer's family. "I want you to take my phone. I haven't heard anything else from the guard, so I hung up, but more people are going to call. I already sent the group text we decided on to let everyone know what's happening and to stay away. Just keep an eye on the phone for me, will you?"

"Anything you need," Meyer promised.

Ollis was down to his underwear, but he paused to grab the back of Meyer's neck and pull him close. "I need you to be safe and survive," Ollis said. "Can you do that for me?"

"Only if you do the same for me. We'll both be safe and come home at the end of this, all right?"

Ollis kissed Meyer hard. Meyer wanted more. He wanted to shield Ollis from the horrors of the world, from having to fight people he'd once considered pack, but he couldn't. These wolves had made their decision, and everyone would pay the consequences. Unfortunately, that included Ollis.

Ollis stepped back, tugged off his underwear, and shifted after handing his phone to Meyer. Meyer stuck it into his pocket so he wouldn't lose it. He had to resist the urge to grab Ollis and pull him back when Ollis ran for the trees. Instead, he grabbed his sword from the porch and ran after him.

His family followed. It was good to know that he and Ollis wouldn't be fighting alone, and more people would arrive. Ollis had planned for this with Kieran and Sloan, so everyone who was able to defend themselves and the pack would be there. Unfortunately, that wouldn't include Merrick, Kieran, and Sloan, but they still had plenty of people, and Meyer was sure it would be enough for them to win. Unless Kieran's sister had recruited another pack, this would be fairly easy.

Meyer prayed it would be.

Ollis was running in front of the family, but Meyer did his best not to be left behind, even though he was nowhere near as fast. He didn't want to think about Ollis throwing himself into a fight without being right behind him. Meyer was ready to sacrifice himself if it meant keeping Ollis safe, but he hoped it wouldn't come to that.

The closer they got, the louder the sound of the fight became. Meyer could smell blood, which made his gums ache, but he ignored it. It was easy when he focused on what he was here to do and who he was protecting.

When they reached the fight, Ollis didn't hesitate. He threw himself into it, knocking down one of the enemy wolves with one strong jump. The wolf turned onto Ollis, letting go of the guard they'd been biting. Meyer was pretty sure the guard was dead, but he nodded at Rex to check while he focused on what was happening to Ollis.

The two wolves rolled. Luckily, they'd planned for this. All the wolves who belonged to the pack wore thick leather collars around their necks. It offered protection from bites, but it also meant that the people who couldn't turn into wolves and couldn't identify pack members by scent wouldn't mistake them for attackers. It also meant that Meyer knew that the wolf Ollis was attacking wasn't a part of the pack anymore. If they had been before, they'd given it up when they'd left with Fay and even more so today.

Ollis pushed the wolf against a tree. Meyer winced at the sound of something loudly breaking, but no matter how much he wanted to focus on his boyfriend, he couldn't.

Another wolf ran toward him. There was no collar around their neck, so Meyer knew they weren't a pack member.

He raised his sword and got ready to defend himself and the people he loved.

Meyer did his best to stay close to Ollis. It wasn't just because he wanted to defend him, although that was a big part of it. But Ollis was the alpha, which meant he'd be a prime target for these wolves. If they wanted control of the pack, taking Ollis out would be the best way to get it.

People were fighting everywhere around Meyer. More pack members had arrived, but unfortunately, so had more enemy wolves. It looked like Fay had found more allies. Meyer hated that. He wanted to find her, give her a good shake, and ask how she dared attack the people she was supposed to care about, but he wasn't even sure she was present.

That changed quickly. When one of the wolves came to stand in front of a panting Ollis, Meyer knew they were in trouble.

The wolf shifted, and there stood Fay. With her chin held high, she almost looked regal, but Meyer knew the darkness in her heart. She wasn't a queen. She wasn't even a good alpha. She only cared about herself and her power, and if she ever got control of the pack, things wouldn't end well for the wolves.

"You're still in time to surrender," she drawled. She opened her arms. "Look around you. You're going to lose, Ollis. We both know it."

She might be right. Even with a dragon shifter on their side, things weren't looking good. Ollis was bleeding from a gash in his side, and Meyer had been bitten several times. The wounds pulsed and hurt, but he did his best to ignore them.

"What are you fighting for?" Fay asked. "What did my brother promise you? I'll give you everything he would and more if you surrender and hand over the pack right now."

Meyer wondered how well Fay knew Ollis. She wouldn't have said any of that if she knew him at all because she would have known his answer would always be no. He'd made a promise to Kieran. He'd sworn he'd keep the pack safe, and that was what he'd do to the best of his ability. Surrendering to Kieran's sister wouldn't be keeping the pack safe but only himself, which was why there was no way Ollis would do it.

Fay stepped closer. "Come on, Ollis. Remember when we were kids? I liked you because you were nice and sweet, and I bet you still are. That's not how an alpha is supposed to be. Alphas aren't nice and sweet. You did your best but failed, and no one will hold that against you. You can save the pack. My brother isn't here to save you. He left, and you no longer have to be loyal to him. You can be loyal to me. If you are, I'll make sure you never have to fight again."

It was an interesting proposition, but Meyer already knew what Ollis's answer would be.

He grinned when Ollis shifted. His boyfriend was about to send Fay to hell, and Meyer couldn't wait to see it.

Ollis panted through his shift. He should probably stay in his wolf form, but he wanted to tell Fay to fuck off to her face instead of just thinking it.

His entire body hurt. He was used to fighting, although most of the time, it happened during training. He was a guard, so he was fit for fighting, but he'd never had to deal with anything like this.

He forced himself to look around, even though he didn't want to see the devastation. It didn't look good. There were so many bodies and wounded that it was hard to tell which side had more victims. It was clear that Fay had found allies, and their number was almost enough for the pack to have to surrender.

Almost, but not quite. Ollis wouldn't surrender. He and Kieran had talked about it, and they'd agreed. Surrendering wouldn't help anyone, especially not the pack. Fay would get her revenge on the people she felt had betrayed her, so it would be best for them to go down fighting.

Which was what Ollis was planning on doing.

He stood up taller and tried not to look at the many bodies littering the ground around him. Some of them had collars around their necks, so he knew the pack had lost members. He felt like most fallen wolves didn't have one, but he couldn't tell.

"There you are," Fay said.

She sounded satisfied, and it took everything Ollis had not to jump forward. He didn't care that she was a woman or the old alpha's daughter. She was evil, and he wanted her away from his pack.

"Why are you doing this?" he asked, even though he already knew the answer.

"The pack is mine," Fay said with a snarl. "Kieran stole it, and I'm here to take it back."

"And you think I'm going to surrender?"

"You better if you don't want to die." She gave him a toothy smile. "Although that could be arranged, too, depending on how loyal you are to my brother. Do you want to die, Ollis? Do you want to watch the people you're supposed to protect die because of you?"

Ollis snorted. "You're saying you'll stop this fight if I surrender?"

"Yes. I just want the pack back. I don't want my people to die, even though they abandoned me and my father."

More probably, she didn't want them to die because if they did, what kind of pack would she have left? Saying it out loud wouldn't be a good idea, but Ollis was done with good ideas. He'd done everything he could. He'd put the plan into motion, so he knew Kieran and the others were coming back. He only had to resist for a bit longer, and then Kieran would be here, and he'd know what to do.

Ollis looked sideways at Meyer, who'd never left his side. He hated seeing the many bite marks on Meyer's arms and hands. There was even one bleeding on his calf, and Ollis wanted to find the wolf who had bitten him and do the same to them.

He'd seen how Meyer had defended himself. The result was all around him. How many of the fallen wolves had been skewered by Meyer's sword?

Watching Meyer fight with his sword was really fucking hot, and Ollis wished the circumstances weren't so dire. Maybe he could ask Meyer to take out his sword and show him how good he was with it when they were alone in Ollis's house.

But before they could do that, Ollis had something to do.

He turned his attention back to Fay. He was sure that his disgust for her was clear in his expression because she didn't look happy. Either that or she could tell he wasn't about to surrender.

"I'm not helping you do this," he told her. "You'd be an awful alpha. Just look at what you're doing. You're killing people you should want to protect. Who would want you as their alpha when you're so ready to do something like this? When you're throwing a tantrum about your brother taking the pack away from you? You're nothing more than a little girl, Fay, and your place isn't at the head of any pack."

There. Ollis had told her what he thought of her. He was standing his ground. It would probably cause his death, but he didn't care. He'd die knowing he'd done the right thing and had defended his people, which was what he'd expected to happen.

He just hated that Meyer and his family were suffering along with him. He would have tried to convince them to leave if he'd thought he'd have had a chance. They'd become pack members, but this still wasn't their fight. Ollis hated to believe that their long lives might be cut short because of Fay and how power-hungry she was.

But there would be no convincing them to run. They'd made their choice, just like Ollis.

Fay screeched and shifted. Ollis did the same, but she was faster and threw herself at him. He withstood the attack, knowing he needed to show his pack that he was ready to protect them with his life.

He was. He'd never expected to die like this, but maybe he should have, especially after this mess had started. He wasn't sure what to think of the fact that it would be Fay who would kill him rather than a dragon, but that was all right, he supposed. At least he knew Fay. Maybe she'd eventually come to regret killing him.

He almost snorted as he tried pushing her away. She wouldn't regret any of this. She didn't care about Ollis or that they'd grown up together. She only cared about herself.

She bit Ollis's shoulder, and he howled. He kicked his legs against her stomach, clawing bloody wounds into the soft skin, but she didn't let go. For a moment, Ollis wondered why no one was coming to help him. He didn't dare look around, but he could hear people fighting. If Meyer was free to move, he'd already have pulled Fay off Ollis, which meant he was busy defending himself and that Ollis was on his own.

Fay's fangs in Ollis's shoulder fucking hurt, but as long as she was biting him there, it meant she couldn't go for the throat. It gave him a little bit of space, and he had to use it as well as he could. He might be wearing a collar, but he wouldn't put it past her to find a way around it.

He scratched his back legs against Fay's stomach again, pushing harder this time. He dug his nails into her skin, hoping she'd let go of his shoulder to defend herself. If she didn't move, he might manage to wound her deeply, which could be a deadly end to this fight.

Something silver flashed above Ollis's head. He tried jerking back, but Fay still had her fangs clamped into him, and the movement made him howl in pain. The sword embedded itself into Fay's back, and she finally let go as her eyes widened.

She stumbled back, and Ollis scrambled out of the way. He was just in time to see Meyer let go of his sword that was still planted in Fay's back and grab her around the neck. He hauled her up as if she weighed nothing, bearing his fangs at her even though she couldn't see them since she was turned toward Ollis.

That was why she didn't see the bite coming. Ollis did,

though, and he watched with wide eyes as Meyer bit Fay's neck.

It couldn't be easy. Fay was in her wolf form. The fur meant her neck was partly protected, but Meyer didn't seem to care. He held her in place, using both of his arms so she didn't move.

Ollis couldn't look away. He got to his paws, but his legs shook. He could feel he was bleeding from his shoulder, but that wasn't what mattered the most now.

He shifted. Meyer was still drinking from Fay, and while Ollis didn't feel sorry for her, he didn't want Meyer to feel bad. He'd told Ollis he always tried not to hurt people when he fed, which was why he was happy to drink from blood bags, but if he didn't let go, he would hurt Fay.

The sound of wings made Ollis look up. A dragon was flying above them, trying to find a way to come lower. There was only one of them, so Ollis was pretty sure it wasn't the clan, but he was still tense. His attention was torn between Meyer and the dragon and remained that way until the dragon finally landed. There was someone on his back, and Ollis breathed easier when Parker hopped off and the dragon turned into Luca.

That got Meyer's attention. He dropped Fay's body, and at that moment, he looked like the vampires in horror movies. Blood dripped from his mouth, and his eyes were wild.

He moved toward Luca, and Ollis knew he needed to do something before things escalated. Meyer wouldn't normally hurt Luca, but the situation was far from normal. Just in case, Ollis placed himself between Meyer and Luca, looking at his boyfriend and raising both of his hands to press against Meyer's chest.

"He's on our side, remember?" he said.

Meyer blinked as if he couldn't understand what Ollis was saying, and for a moment, Ollis was terrified that he couldn't.

He'd heard about bloodlust, but he didn't know if it was real. He didn't want it to be.

Meyer blinked again, and finally, he was back. Ollis relaxed and almost fell forward in his haste to wrap himself around Meyer. "You're all right," he murmured.

Meyer's body was tense. "I killed her," he mumbled.

Ollis leaned back. "You did, and no one is going to miss her. You did what you had to do to protect me."

"I'm not sure Kieran will agree."

"I *know* he will. We defeated her, Meyer, and it's thanks to you."

Ollis looked around. With Fay gone, it seemed like most of the wolves she'd brought with her had either surrendered or run. The only ones left behind were the bodies and the wounded.

The pack had won, but at what cost?

CHAPTER SEVEN

"Meyer glared at him. "I don't care where she bit you. You're on bed rest, and that's that."

"I could at least meet with people. Kieran and Sloan's job isn't done, which means they still need me."

"And you need rest after being attacked by Fay and having to defend the pack. Kieran agreed, which is why he's been meeting with people instead of you. Your only focus needs to be resting and healing."

Meyer didn't think he'd ever forget the moment he'd realized that if he didn't do something, Ollis would die. He'd been fighting a wolf, but his mind had been on Fay and Ollis. When he'd turned after sending the wolf running, it had been to see Fay biting Ollis. There had been blood everywhere, and part of Meyer's brain had broken. The only thing he'd been able to think of was that he had to save Ollis, and a vampire's greatest weapon was their fangs.

He still remembered the feeling of fur in his mouth and the taste of Fay's blood. It gave him nightmares, and not because it was wolf shifter blood. He liked Ollis's blood just fine, but he hadn't been biting Ollis.

When he bit Ollis, there was no fur involved.

Meyer hoped he'd be able to forget all of this in time, but he doubted it. It had only been a few days, and the horror still plagued him. He didn't regret killing Fay, although he wasn't sure where that left him with Kieran and the pack. She'd been a danger, and not just to Ollis. Taking her out hopefully meant that the wolves who'd left the pack would stop attacking, although Meyer wouldn't put it past Kieran's father to decide he wanted his pack back and try something. His daughter had just died, though, so even if he did try to get back at Kieran, it would probably take him some time to do so.

"I *am* resting. You're making sure that."

Meyer was. That was why he'd moved Ollis into his room. Ollis had wanted to go home, but Meyer wanted him here, and not only because it was easier to keep an eye on him. Here at the house, many people would help if he needed anything. He just had to shout, and Meyer's family would help.

They hadn't had the opportunity to do so yet because Meyer hadn't left Ollis's side.

A knock on the door made him frown. He'd told his family to leave Ollis alone so he could rest, but he wouldn't put it past a few of them to decide Ollis needed company. Meyer was ready to tell them to fuck off, but he didn't because when he opened, he found his father standing there rather than one of his siblings.

"Kieran is here to see you and Ollis," he said.

Kieran was the one person Meyer couldn't kick out of the house. As the alpha, he had every right to be here, especially after what had happened and considering who Ollis was.

Meyer wasn't looking forward to talking to him. Kieran could be here to kick him out of the pack. Fay had been a cruel asshole, but she was still Kieran's sister, and she was very much dead.

"Let him in," Ollis said. "I want to know how things are going."

There was no saying no to that. Meyer moved toward the window instead of sitting down on the bed with Ollis. He didn't think he'd be able to stay still.

It took Kieran only a handful of minutes to appear at the door. He knocked and peeked inside, smiling at Ollis.

"You look better," he said.

Ollis started to shrug, then seemed to remember that it had hurt like hell the last time he'd tried it. "I feel better, although it would be great if I was allowed to leave the bedroom."

Kieran looked amused. "Is Meyer hovering?"

Meyer felt stiff in a way he never had with Kieran, not even in the very beginning after they'd met. "I'm making sure he has enough rest so that the wound heals as quickly as possible," he said. "You need him, and he wants to come back to work."

"I do need him, but I want him to be healthy more. I'm not worried. I know you'll take good care of him."

Meyer might as well get it out of the way. He wanted to know what was about to happen. He'd scream if he didn't find out soon, and no one wanted that. "I apologize for what happened with your sister," he said, fully turning toward Kieran. "I shouldn't have killed her."

Kieran examined Meyer for a moment. Meyer wondered what he saw in him. His sister's murderer?

"You did it to save Ollis and the pack," Kieran said. "I can't blame you for that. Besides, if you'd captured her instead of killed her, she would have died anyway. That's what happens to traitors. She was too dangerous to the pack, so I couldn't have let her live. You did me a favor."

Meyer snorted. "I killed your sister."

"Exactly. As the alpha, I would have been expected to decide her fate if she'd still been alive when I got there. I would have had to decide she needed to die and to say so to her face. No matter how much she'd changed, she was still my sister. I don't want you to worry about what you did, Meyer. She wasn't the sister I grew up with anymore. I couldn't recognize her, and I'm glad I won't have to see her like that ever again."

Meyer wasn't sure he believed he'd done Kieran a favor, but it didn't look like the alpha was going to kick him out, so maybe it didn't matter. Besides, he agreed. It was best for Fay to be dead because if she wasn't, she'd find another way to get to the pack, and they already had enough problems with the clan.

"Do we know what happened?" Ollis asked. "Meyer has been keeping me out of the loop. I get that he's worried about me and wants me to rest, but it's driving me nuts. I need to know what happened when you got back and with the hydra plan."

Kieran sat in the chair by the bed. "From what we gathered from Fay's survivors, they had spies keeping an eye on the pack at all times. When they saw Sloan and me leave, they called her, and she decided to attack. She didn't go to the clan, even though she was supposed to. She took matters into her own hands, and as we know, it didn't end well. I don't know how the clan took it, but I doubt they're heartbroken over her death. They were using her, but they never cared about her."

Initially, Meyer hadn't understood why the clan would want to ally with Fay, but then he'd realized that it gave them cannon fodder. They could use the wolves because they didn't care if they died.

Which was precisely what happened.

"As for the hydra shifters, the meeting went well. They agreed to help protect the area from the clan, although we still don't know what that will look like. They understand that eventually, the dragons will target them, too. Luckily, they come with more allies, and I can't begin to tell you how relieved I am that we're finally not facing this alone."

Meyer went to sit next to Ollis on the bed. He wasn't nervous anymore. He wouldn't be asked to leave, so he could make sure Ollis healed and protect him when the time came.

Ollis leaned against Meyer as soon as he settled in next to him. *This* was why Meyer hadn't hesitated to kill Fay. She'd hurt Ollis, and if Meyer hadn't stepped in, she would have killed him. Now, she would never hurt anyone ever again, and knowing that was enough that Meyer didn't think he would ever regret killing her.

Their world was harsh, as he'd learned a long time ago. He had many people to protect, and he'd do it in any way he saw fit. Luckily, it seemed that Kieran understood that. Meyer didn't want to lose his friendship, and he definitely didn't want to lose the pack.

He wouldn't. The only people who could take the pack away from him was the clan, and while there was a good chance they'd do just that, Meyer, Ollis, and everyone else would do the same thing they'd done against Fay.

They'd stand their ground and fight.

About the Author

Catherine is the creator of several series, most of them paranormal, including the Whitedell Pride Series and the Gillham Pack Series. While she graduated in translation, she decided to go the writer's way because it was more fun to create her own stories and characters.

She's been living in Italy for more than twenty years, but she's a daughter of the North—Belgium to be precise—and she misses it so much that she's already planning to move back.

She loves pizza—probably too much—her son, her pets, and of course, books. She sneaks some reading time into her schedule every time she has five minutes free from writing, demands from her various pets and son, and lastly, housework.

Connect with her:

lievens.catherine@gmail.com
BookBub: https://www.bookbub.com/authors/catherine-lievens
Website: https://authorcatherinelievens.com/
Facebook: https://www.facebook.com/catherine.lievens.9
Facebook Group: https://www.facebook.com/groups/411788002341528/
Twitter: https://twitter.com/authorCLievens
Newsletter: http://eepurl.com/c-uvKn

www.ingramcontent.com/pod-product-compliance
Lightning Source LLC
LaVergne TN
LVHW020641100826
845148LV00012B/2277

* 9 7 8 1 4 8 7 4 4 1 4 9 4 *